THE BRIDES OF BELLA LUCIA

A family torn apart by secrets, reunited by marriage

When William Valentine returned from the war, as a testament to his love for his beautiful Italian wife, Lucia, he opened the first Bella Lucia restaurant in London. The future looked bright, and William had, he thought, the perfect family.

Now William is nearly ninety, and not long for this world, but he has three top London restaurants with prime spots throughout Knightsbridge and the West End. He has two sons, John and Robert, and grown-up grandchildren on both sides of the Atlantic who are poised to take this small gastronomic success story into the twenty-first century.

But when William dies, and the family fight to control the destiny of the Bella Lucia business, they discover a multitude of long-buried secrets, scandals, the threat of financial ruin and, ultimately, two great loves they hadn't even dreamed of: the love of a lifelong partner, and the love of a family reunited….

It's a trip to the Outback, where secrets
are revealed this month, in…
***Wanted: Outback Wife* by Ally Blake**

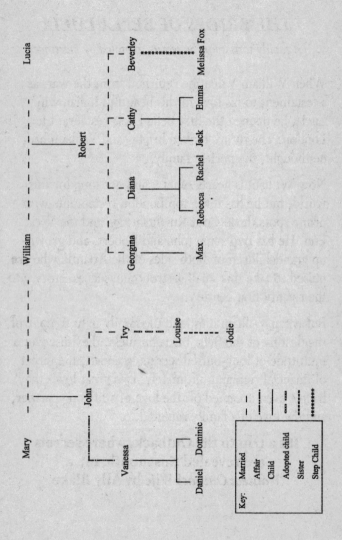

Key:
- Married: - - - - -
- Affair: ••••••••••
- Child: ———
- Adopted child: - - -
- Sister: — — —
- Step Child: ✳✳✳✳✳✳✳✳

Mary - - - John - - - Ivy - - - Louise - - - Jodie

Vanessa

Daniel   Dominic

William - - - Lucia

Robert

Georgina   Diana   Cathy   Beverley ✳✳✳✳✳✳✳✳ Melissa Fox

Max   Rebecca   Rachel   Jack   Emma

ALLY BLAKE
Wanted: Outback Wife

TORONTO • NEW YORK • LONDON
AMSTERDAM • PARIS • SYDNEY • HAMBURG
STOCKHOLM • ATHENS • TOKYO • MILAN • MADRID
PRAGUE • WARSAW • BUDAPEST • AUCKLAND

ISBN-13: 978-0-373-18262-6
ISBN-10:   0-373-18262-7

WANTED: OUTBACK WIFE

First North American Publication 2006.

Copyright © 2006 by Harlequin Books S.A.

Special thanks and acknowledgment are given to Ally Blake for her contribution to *The Brides of Bella Lucia* series.

THE BRIDES OF BELLA LUCIA
A family torn apart by secrets, reunited by marriage

**First there was double
the excitement as we met twins
Rebecca and Rachel Valentine**

Having the Frenchman's Baby, Rebecca Winters
Coming Home to the Cowboy, Patricia Thayer

**Then we joined Emma Valentine as she
got a royal welcome this September**

The Rebel Prince, Raye Morgan

**Now, take a trip to the Outback and meet
Louise Valentine's long-lost sister, Jodie**

Wanted: Outback Wife, Ally Blake

**On cold November nights catch up
with newcomer Daniel Valentine**

Married Under the Mistletoe, Linda Goodnight

**Snuggle up with sexy Jack Valentine
over Christmas**

Crazy About the Boss, Teresa Southwick

**In the New Year join Melissa as she
heads off to a desert kingdom**

The Nanny and the Sheikh, Barbara McMahon

**And don't miss the thrilling end to the
Valentine saga in February**

The Valentine Bride, Liz Fielding

To my Sirens—Hulda, Nic, Ola, and
Trish—for being the best listeners, huggers,
and champions a girl could ever want.
Smoochy kisses.

CHAPTER ONE

HAPPY hour at The Cave was drawing to a close, but Jodie didn't mind at all.

She had used up every second of employment her working visa had allowed so now her final weeks in Melbourne were hers to do with as she pleased. And it pleased her to sit on a bar stool twirling a daisy-shaped earring she had made from scratch earlier that day, sharing a bottle of red wine that someone else had paid for, and enjoying every last second that she wasn't in London.

'Where's Mandy?' her housemate Lisa asked. 'I have to start work in eight minutes and those customers who haven't booked a table won't turn themselves away.'

'*Beach Street* is back on in less than three minutes,' Louise added, her clipped London accent so obvious amongst the neighbouring Aussie strine. 'No matter how exiting Mandy's big surprise, after the break Angelo is about to find out that

Cait was once married to his brother, so her announcement will be nothing but white noise to me.'

'She'll be here,' Jodie said chirpily. The fact that Louise, the half-sister she had never even known existed until two weeks before, had turned up on her doorstep amidst her *own* family drama wasn't lost on Jodie. But she began throwing pretzel chunks at Louise, who was glancing at the overhead television every few seconds, all the same.

'If you do that one more time, Jodie,' Louise warned, 'when the next ad break comes along I will retaliate.'

Jodie grinned, but she stopped throwing pretzels at Louise and threw one into her mouth instead, amazed anew that this tall, cool, sophisticated, blonde product of the infamous restaurant family, the Valentines of London, was related to her—mousy little Jodie Simpson.

It was obvious Louise got the glamour goods from their shared mother, whereas Jodie wasn't sure what she had acquired from Patricia except a lifelong pain in the neck. But thankfully all that was back in London, far far away from friends and fun on this fine Melbourne evening.

'I've got it!' Mandy cried out, rushing in as fast as her pencil-thin power skirt and two-inch heels would allow. She waved a piece of paper high above her head.

'If that's a doctor's certificate telling you rotten Jake has finally given you something only penicillin will cure, I don't want to know about it,' Lisa called back.

'Funny,' Mandy said. 'Now leave my love life out of this; this magical piece of paper is all about Jodie's.'

'*My* love life?' Jodie wheezed while coughing up a pretzel crumb that had lodged in her throat.

'Yep,' Mandy said. 'I have found a way for you to stay in Australia.'

That got everyone's attention. Lisa stopped staring at her watch. Jodie's mouth went so dry she wouldn't have had a clue if she had been drinking red wine or juiced sawdust. Louise spun on her seat leaving *Beach Street*'s Angelo and Cait to sort out their worries on their own.

Jodie felt a pang of guilt lodge between her shoulder blades. Until that moment Louise had had no idea that she was considering not returning to London. In Jodie Louise would have a close friend outside the Valentine family she was feeling so angry toward right now, and a sister to be at her side when she met her real mother for the first time.

And though Jodie so wanted to be that person for Louise, she wanted to be in Melbourne more.

She waved a quick hand at Louise, intimating she would explain everything later.

'How? I've tried everything,' Jodie managed, 'including writing letters to the Australian Department of Immigration telling them how much I want to be one of you.'

Jodie looked from Mandy to Lisa. She would have given her right ear to be like them—bright, breezy, and free as the wind. And being that way in Melbourne.

'But I still have to be on a plane back to London on the thirtieth of December,' Jodie said, letting her hand flop back to the table.

Mandy grinned. 'I have found a way.'

'And it has something to do with Jodie's love life?' Louise asked, sounding anxious.

Mandy nodded. 'Dust off your best bridesmaid's frock; we are going to marry your sister off to an Australian.'

Jodie felt herself blanch and blush all at once. 'You want to *marry me...off*?'

Mandy looked down at the computer printout she held through a pair of tiny reading glasses. 'The marriage would only have to last two years. At first you'll get a Temporary Spouse Visa and at the end of those two years, once you achieve your Permanent Visa, you can divorce the guy and be free.'

Free. Of all the words Mandy could have chosen to sell the idea that was the one that worked. For a child from a split home it certainly rang in her ears a lot more comfortably than marriage, or divorce…

But surely it couldn't be that simple.

'You and Lisa are both natives, yet Lisa has been single since I've known her and the closest thing to a long-term boyfriend you have managed to locate is rotten Jake. What makes you think I can do it in two and a half months?'

Lisa looked back down at her watch again, neatly avoiding Jodie's comment.

'One and a half,' Mandy said, also ignoring the point.

'Excuse me?'

'You have to fill out an Intention To Marry form one month and one day before marrying. So at the outside, you have six weeks in which to find your man. Considering it has been a month since you starting putting big red crosses on your calendar in a passive-aggressive reminder of the looming Day You Have To Leave, I had my team make it top priority. As of today you have your own website!'

'Website?' Jodie repeated.

'It's called www.ahusbandinahurry.com,' Mandy said, puffing up proudly.

Louise, who had been elegantly sipping on a Cosmopolitan, coughed inelegantly into her drink.

Jodie sunk her head onto her hands so as not to see the amplified mortification that would surely be in Louise's eyes. 'But what if anyone I know has seen it? What if my *mother* has seen it?'

'Unless she is trawling the Internet looking for a cute British bride, then I think you'll be fine. Besides, we did you proud. We used that photo of you from the Christmas in July barbecue on the home page.'

'Not the action shot where I was laughing so hard you could see my tonsils as I fell off my chair by way of too much champagne?' Jodie asked.

'That's the one,' Mandy said, grinning. 'The men at work voted that one their favourite. They all said you seemed, and I quote: "cute, adorable, and fun".'

'So why not just set her up with one of the guys from your work?' Louise asked. Several faint frown lines marred her forehead. She wasn't as aloof to the situation as she was making out. But Jodie couldn't deal with what those frown lines meant. Not yet.

Jodie was beginning to see the possibilities. There was any number of reasons why two people could happily marry for convenience's sake. And considering this was her last chance at staying in Australia, the place where she had found fabulous friends, a growing number of people who stopped her on the street to ask her where they could buy the unique floral-inspired earrings she herself created, and where she had begun to delight in her youth, maybe, just maybe, she could pull this off.

That was the clincher. After years of being the adult in the family, the one who remembered to pick up milk, the one who kept the house free of dust bunnies, the one who remembered to pay the gas bill, the one who made sure her mum got to work in time—when she managed to hold down a job—Jodie felt hopeful that at last she had a chance to find the youth inside herself.

'Oh, no,' Mandy said, 'once they knew she was looking for a husband, even a two-year one, they backed away like I had pulled a shotgun.'

And there was the rub.

Jodie looked to Lisa, who had been quiet through all of this. 'What do you think?'

Lisa held up both hands before slipping off the seat and backing away. 'You don't want to know what I think. Besides, can't talk, I'm now on the clock.'

'She has some old-fashioned view that you should only date, marry, sleep with a guy if you're in love.' Mandy shivered as though that would have saved her from a whole lot of fun. 'But I'm not expecting you to worry about any of that. Leave it all to me.'

Jodie had every intention of leaving it all to Mandy. Though it wasn't in her make-up to come out and say it, she needed help. For there was no way on God's green earth she was ever going back to London. To that oppressive apartment. To that half life…

But the real question was: what sort of man would give up two years of his life to marry her, to be her husband, after knowing her for less than a month?

Heath swung back and forth on the love seat on the veranda of his big old home, staring out across the flat red dirt of Jamesons Run.

A blood-red sunset glowed across the plain. A nimble dry wind whipped along the dusty ground so that the golden kangaroo grass seemed to be waving toward the grand old willow dipping its sad leaves into the dam at the centre of his main paddock.

He could do with rain—and not just to damp down the dust storms that were springing up from nowhere more often than not these days. Rain would be a break in routine of stifling hot temperatures that spoke of an oppressive summer to come. Rain would be a change.

'Knock, knock.'

Heath looked over his shoulder to find his older sister Elena standing in the doorway with a paper plate drooping under the weight of mixed desserts. An outfit of a floral dress and stockings on such a warm day could only mean one thing— a wedding or a funeral. And there had not been a wedding at Jamesons Run in years.

He let his riding-boot-clad feet drag against the wooden floor until the seat stopped swinging so she could sit beside him.

'I brought this for you before the Crabbe sisters had the chance,' Elena said. 'No doubt they are still squabbling over whether you might prefer Carol's custard tart or Rachel's mud cake.'

Heath smiled, and he only hoped he had managed to make it reach his eyes. His appetite seemed to have departed him since the moment he had picked up the phone four days earlier to learn that Marissa was gone, but he swallowed a bite of Elena's home-made pavlova to keep her happy. His mouth was so dry that the sticky passion-fruit topping caught on his palate. Now he would be prying pavlova loose with his heavy tongue all night.

'How you doing, little brother?' Elena asked, patting him on the knee. 'You holding up okay?'

He nodded, though he turned away for a brief moment so she wouldn't see his frown. Why was she worried about him? Cameron was the one she should have been comforting. Cameron was the one who had lost his wife. He had only lost... what? A friend? His last remaining link to the life he had once thought he might have?

'Do we have enough ice?' he asked, tidily avoiding the question. 'I can run into town to get more.'

'We have plenty of ice,' Elena said. Her patting stopped. 'Though I'm sure it won't occur to Cameron to thank you, he appreciates you holding Marissa's wake here. And when you took over for him during the eulogy, oh, that fair broke my heart then and there. You're a good kid, Heath.'

'A thirty-six-year-old kid,' he reminded her. 'Which makes you—'

'A lady of indiscriminate age,' Elena said, cutting him off quick smart. 'So when are we going to get to use this big old place for more than Christmas parties, local community meetings and funerals? When do we all get to come here to celebrate your wedding?'

'Ha! I'm surprised you and the Crabbe sisters haven't lined Cam and me up for a double wedding by now.'

As soon as the words left his mouth he regretted them. They were cruel and hurtful and born of the fact that he barely believed the words even

as he said them. He stood and moved to the edge
of the veranda, wrapping his hands around the
wooden railing until a bunch of splinters poked
deep enough to hurt.

'Sorry,' he said. 'That was out of order.'

'And completely understandable, considering.
Does the thought of settling down frighten you
that much?'

Settling down? That was what she thought had
kept him from the altar all this time? He had
settled down a decade ago. What scared him was
that if one day he settled down at Jamesons Run
with someone else it meant that he would never
leave. But now, on this tragic day, it no longer
seemed the biggest problem in his life.

'What if I told you that right this moment I am
feeling the very opposite?' he said. He turned and
leant his backside against the railing and folded
his arms and stared his big sister down.

'Well, kid, I would say thank the gods.' She
stood and grabbed him by the arms, giving him a
big kiss on the cheek. 'Is there a particular woman
who has brought about this change of heart?'

One woman? Absolutely. But she was gone
now. Not just gone from his life, but gone from all
life. And it had taken a shock of that magnitude
to knock him from the path of his life.

'None in particular,' he said. His reasons were his

to wrangle alone. 'So what do you think? Should I go and give the Crabbe sisters the fright of their life by proposing to one of them right now?'

The Crabbe girls were as sensible a choice as any. He knew from past experience of country-dance bottom-pinching, all instigated by one or the other of them, that they would not have been immune to such an idea. But no matter how hard he tried to picture himself in the role of doting husband with a good little country wife by his side, he found he in all good conscience could not. It felt like too much of the same.

And what he craved so deeply was change.

'No need,' Elena said, reaching into her purse for a pile of yellowed, creased A4 paper. 'I've already signed you up to some dating websites, just in case.'

'Websites?' Heath parroted back. 'Aren't they all just fronts for three-hundred-pound, sixty-year-old Russians looking to relocate?'

Elena's responding sigh was melodramatic. 'I'll have you know over half all new relationships forged by people in their thirties come from meeting over the Internet.'

After a pause, Heath said, 'You just made that up.'

'I did. But it sounds good, don't you think? Now I've found some girls I like, and some I *know* you'll like. All are Melbourne women. Twenty-seven to

thirty-five. Single. Looking for love, not just fun.'
She glanced at him through narrowed eyes.

He took the pages, skimming through pictures
and vital statistics of a dozen perfectly attractive
young women.

One page about halfway through had stuck to
another with a glob of baby food. It caught his eye
for the fact that it had a big red cross through it.
Why, he had no idea, for the woman in the picture
looked absolutely worth investigating.

She was laughing so hard he could almost feel
the energy radiating from the page. Something
about the angle of the photo made him feel kind
of dizzy, as if he were about to tip over if he didn't
plant his feet.

Behind the smile was English-rose skin. Huge
jade-green cat's eyes. Long curling eyelashes. A
fine chin and a nice straight nose. And she had a
seriously sexy stash of strawberry-blonde waves.
She barely looked twenty but there was something steely behind her pretty green eyes that had
Heath thinking that she was older.

A bulleted list below the photo told him she
hated chocolate, her favourite colour was yellow,
she cooked a mean plate of fettuccini carbonara,
and she lived for mascarpone.

Considering he couldn't go a day without chocolate, he wasn't entirely sure he had a favourite

colour, he couldn't eat starch and didn't even know what a mascarpone was, it seemed that they were likely the least-suited pair on the planet. Maybe that was why Elena had crossed her out.

But there was something in those flinty green eyes that kept him staring at her picture. 'What's wrong with this one?' he asked.

Elena glanced at the page and screwed up her nose. 'That one wasn't meant to be there.' She reached out to take it back, but Heath moved it just out of her way.

'Why not?'

'She is the star turn on a website called www.a-husbandinahurry.com. I don't think that bodes well.'

'Don't you think that's what many of these women are after? At least she's honest,' he said. And if he was honest, it was what he wanted too. Now. As soon as possible. A wife. A partner. Someone else with whom to share his space, his time, his life. It was time for him to stop playing it safe. It was time for him to take a risk.

Elena shrugged, obviously not pleased that it hadn't gone all her way. Likely she had picked out a bunch of women who enjoyed cross-stitch and watching car racing on TV so that if all went well she could have a new friend as well as a sister-in-law.

But *that one*, as Elena called her, was different.

Behind the pretty green eyes Heath knew there was fire. And though all week he had been wishing for rain, suddenly fire held a heck of a lot more possibilities. Change was in the air. Barely there, but there all the same. Enough that he could taste it—sweet and welcome on his tongue.

'Heath, are you out here?' a male voice called from inside. His youngest brother, Caleb.

'Out here, buddy.'

'Someone knocked over the punch bowl and there's pineapple pieces swimming all over the dining-room floor.'

He let out a long slow breath and bit back the suggestion that Caleb could have cleaned the thing up himself. But the kid was spoilt. All of his siblings were. And it was his fault.

But inside there were worse things afoot than pineapple on the floor. His brother Cameron was doing his best to keep himself from shattering into a million pieces while trying to help his two little daughters understand why their mummy was not coming home. And big brother Heath was hiding outside.

Well, not any more. 'I'm coming, Caleb.'

'To save the day as always, bro,' Caleb said, slapping Heath on the back, but Heath was sure the kid had no notion of how true that was.

* * *

On a balmy Saturday night, two weeks later, Jodie angled her beloved twenty-year-old car, aptly nicknamed Rusty, into an empty car park in a side street off Flinders. She threw a handful of coins into the parking meter as she spied a gap in Saturday-night traffic cruising the length of the grand old train station. She hitched her black sparkly halter an inch higher and tugged her tight jeans an inch lower and ran as fast as her borrowed high heels would carry her.

She was late, as an hour before she could still have been found sitting on the couch with Louise in her pyjama bottoms, Chelsea Football Club T-shirt and slippers, as she hadn't entirely been planning on turning up that night.

Over the past two weeks, Jodie had met twelve different guys that she and Mandy had chosen from the responses to her website. An actor, a vet, a guy who sold mobile phone contracts door-to-door, and a funeral director whose massive Adam's apple slid up and down in his throat with such vigour Jodie had found it hard to look anywhere else. And she would have put every cent she owned on the fact that most had come for a good time, not a long time.

What was she doing interviewing prospective husbands? Really? When Jodie reached the safety of the footpath, she closed her eyes and visualised waving goodbye to Mandy and Lisa, getting on the jumbo plane, landing in Heathrow, catching the tube, knocking on the front door of the tiny flat she had shared with her mother for twenty-five years... No, if she was to have any sort of life, she had to stay the course.

Jodie pushed open the heavy carved door nestled into the underbelly of the train station and rushed down the carpeted steps.

Lisa, the *maître d'* at the popular restaurant, grimaced as she came into view. 'Another minute and I would have given away your table.'

'I probably would have thanked you if you had,' Jodie muttered. 'Is he here yet?'

Lisa shook her head. 'But Mandy is prowling in your corner. Go settle her before she frightens away my customers.'

Jodie gave her a quick pat on the arm before skimming through the tables to the private table for two in the corner. When she saw Mandy sitting in a chair, her stiletto tapping nervously against the floor, Jodie was torn between staying or making a run for it to the ladies' room, squeezing out the tiny window and dropping atop the Dumpster a floor below.

'Nice of you to show,' Mandy said as Jodie slipped quickly into the cool seat across from her.

Jodie took a steadying gulp of Mandy's red

wine before grabbing a bread roll and shoving nibble-sized bites into her nervous mouth. 'Yeah, well, it didn't help that just as I was leaving Scott came over to propose to me.'

'Scott?' Mandy said, her face paling. 'Across the hall *Scott*? Predilection for leather pants and mesh shirts *Scott*? Not quite sure where his right eye is looking *Scott*?'

Jodie nodded along with Mandy's every query. 'Somehow he had found your clever website. His exact words were: "So how about it? You and me—matrimonial bliss?"'

'Please tell me you said no.'

Jodie nodded. But in that brief split second, she had actually considered his offer. He lived across the hall, so she wouldn't have to move far. He had a thing for her, which had been obvious since the day she had moved into the building, so he would do anything to help her out in her plight. But the very fact that he had a thing for her ruled him out even if his goofy oddness did not. It wouldn't be fair.

If she was going to do this thing, she had to do it right. No romantic connections. No complications from the start. The last thing she wanted was for it all to end in tears and broken promises. She'd lived through enough of that when her father had walked out when she was thirteen, so living it up close and personal was not on her agenda.

She had thanked him for his kind offer, but declined. Though compared to her other dates that week he wasn't the bottom of the totem-pole.

'He had settled in to watch *Beach Street* when I left so I had to leave poor Lou behind. I don't trust him not to sneak into my room and try to steal a pair of my underpants again.'

'Right. Good point.'

'So who's the lucky contestant tonight?' Jodie asked on a sigh.

'First up we have Heath.' Mandy flipped through her colour-coded sheets clipped in a neat folder. 'Heath Jameson. The farmer.'

Jodie winced. A farmer, for goodness' sake! The fact that he didn't send an email in the form of a dirty limerick or attach a photo of himself in Speedos put him in the maybe pile. But the thought of moving to a farm for two years was un-inspiring to say the least. She was a city girl, born and bred. She loved the seasons in Melbourne, the food, the culture, the window shopping, the archi-tecture and the friends she had made there. But most of all she liked herself in Melbourne.

But a farm? In the outback? She pictured a barn with a leaking tin roof. A wood-burning fireplace with old copper pots the likes of which she had seen in old Western movies. A mangy work dog sleeping on the end of the double bed that had lumps and bumps worn into it by past generations. And wouldn't she have to get one of those hats with corks hanging all around it to ward off flies?

'Ready?' Mandy asked.

'Ready as I'll ever be.'

'Excellent. After this one, there's two more tonight.'

Two more? She let out a long groan. Suddenly, despite the living distance from the city she loved, so long as the guy was a gentleman and said yes, she decided she would marry him then and there. So long as she could stop all this dreadful dating and see a way to a future down under.

Mandy slipped away into the crowd and Jodie was left sending glances towards the bar. Which one would farm boy turn out to be? The guy in all black flicking lint off his double-breasted jacket? Unlikely. The balding blond in the plaid shirt and jeans picking crumbs out of his teeth with his butter knife? Oh, please, no.

Jodie couldn't help checking her teeth for sesame seeds in the reflection of her bread knife when the front door swished open letting in a flush of warm night air and, with it, a man.

A man with a to-die-for tan, the likes of which

Jodie had only ever seen on school friends just back from the Greek Islands, subconsciously pushing his wind-mussed, dark blond hair somewhat into place. A man with the kind of natural highlights other guys would pay a fortune for. A man in an untucked white shirt over dark denim who gave a friendly half-smile as he caught Lisa's eye at the door.

Jodie knew that second he was hers.

Lisa tossed her long blonde hair as she turned and, with a little finger wave, beckoned the man to follow. And follow he did with a lean, long-legged stride.

'Not bad,' Lisa mouthed as she neared.

As he came closer Jodie saw that this man was just the way she imagined Australian guys ought to be—permanent creases at the corners of his eyes from too much smiling or too much sun, a strong jaw covered in sexy stubble as though he had shaved many hours before, and eyes so blue they made her heart ache.

But she wasn't in this game for heartache. This was to be a purely heart-free and ache-free endeavour.

Jodie scrunched her toes in her high-heeled sandals to force the blood away from her burning cheeks to other parts of her body. The whole 'blushing English rose' thing could be pretty on some girls, but with her auburn hair she felt like a big red blotchy tomato. And the more she panicked about it, the more she blushed.

Suddenly the ladies' room, the tiny window and the Dumpster seemed unreservedly the right choice.

'Can I get you a drink?' Lisa asked as they reached the table.

'Thanks,' he said, his voice a rich, resonant bass. 'A beer would be great.'

Lisa gave him a beaming smile, turned it into a frown for Jodie, then spun on her heel and left. Jodie managed to drag herself to her feet on wobbly knees that almost gave way.

Her companion leaned over and offered her a large, long-fingered hand to shake. 'Good evening, Jodie. I'm Heath Jameson. It's a pleasure to finally meet you.'

CHAPTER TWO

'NICE to finally meet you too, Heath,' Jodie said.

A lively smile lit his eyes. They were so stunning they'd give even Paul Newman a run for his money.

She shook hands. His were work-roughened, but warm. She glanced down, mesmerised by how large and brown his hand was wrapped around her skinny pale fingers. And it was then that she noticed he had a hint of dirt beneath his fingernails.

Of course there was dirt. He was a farmer. Not a city guy. Not a straightforward man looking for a wife to accompany him to work dinners, to get his parents off his back, or to marry quickly to get himself lined up for that work partnership, which was what she figured would bring a man around to her plan. So what on earth was she doing still hanging onto the poor guy's hand?

She let go, and quick, running her hand down the side of her jeans to rub away the tingles. She sat, and her wobbly knees thanked her.

Having broken the ice enough times already that fortnight, she knew how. But while with the others she'd wanted to get down to brass tacks, to lay out the ground rules and find out their motives before even bothering with small talk, with this guy, with this long, lean length of pure and un-adulterated gorgeousness, it felt ridiculous forming the question: *why do you want to marry me?*

Instead she caved and settled on, 'You found this place okay?'

'I did. I drove here directly from the farm and found it a lot sooner than I had expected to.'

'But I just saw you come in the front door.'

A knowing smile in his eyes lit brighter, and she bit her lip. Jodie felt her horrid blush threatening again, so she turned her eyes determinedly to the residual drops of wine in her glass. Red wine, which would only make her feel warmer. She pushed it out of reach behind the tray of bread rolls.

'I've been walking the streets of Melbourne for an hour and a half,' he explained. 'I'm not terribly good at sitting on my hands, and the last thing I wanted to do was wait and have you not show. And now I'm here, I'm really glad you did. Show.'

'I take it I'm not your first blind date,' Jodie said, the unstoppable blotchy blush heating her face another degree.

'Well, actually, no,' he said, a slight hint of pink warming his tanned neck too. She was hard pressed not to sigh. 'And though in the past they have been mostly disastrous, I figured I would try one more time just to find out what the heck mascarpone is.'

She blinked. 'Mascarpone?'

'On your website it said that you lived for it. I knew I couldn't go any further without knowing.'

'Oh. Right. Well, it's a type of Italian cream cheese. In my opinion, a sandwich is simply not a sandwich without mascarpone to hold it all together.'

'Okay, then.' He blinked a few times as he let the info settle and then he laid a huge grin on her. 'I guess I can now go on.'

After the previous candidates, this guy wasn't just a honey to look at, he was polite and nice and saying all the right things. She would be hard pressed to find better. Maybe he was the one.

She flinched so hard at that thought that her elbow slid off the table. Heath even lifted himself off the chair and reached out a hand to her to make sure she was okay. Thankfully at that moment a waitress came over with Heath's beer and another glass of red wine for Jodie so she was saved from extended humiliation.

'So, you're English,' he said once the waitress left.

Feeling more than a little off kilter, Jodie

wrapped her fingers around the stem of her wine-glass. 'Is that a concern?'

'No, not at all. It's just that from the few details on your website I had sort of built up an image of how you would sound, how tall you'd be, that sort of thing.'

Jodie felt herself deflating with every word he spoke. She'd spent years being told by her mother that if only she were taller and not quite so pale she might be pretty. To hear this guy say the same would seal it for sure. 'So how am I different?' she asked, being as she was a glutton for punishment.

Heath blinked, his eye crinkles deepening, as though giving himself a moment to tie all of the pieces in his imagination into a new whole.

'You're smaller somehow. More delicate. And I can't get over that plummy accent.'

Jodie bit at her inner lip, wishing, and not for the first time, that she were a blonde glamazon like Lisa. Or a brunette sex kitten like Mandy. Or serenely elegant like her half-sister Louise. Not wan, wispy, little old her.

'Sorry to disappoint,' she said.

'Not at all,' he said, resting contentedly against the back of his chair as his eyes remained locked onto hers. 'You're lovely.'

Oh, my… Jodie fought the sudden urge to tell him

he was lovely right back. But this wasn't the place, or the time, or the point. She was looking for someone kind, nice, unassuming, and Australian. And added extras along the lines of handsome, charming, and sexy as hell would only complicate things.

'And so are your earrings,' Heath said, catching her unawares by reaching out a curled hand towards her cheek, but stopping a foot from her face and letting his hand drop to the table.

Jodie blinked in surprise. The mere thought of those hands brushing against her ear had robbed her of the power of speech.

Her choice of earrings had been her biggest one of the night. Which of the dozen she had created in a mad productive spurt ought she to choose? Vibrant red glo-mesh ones shaped like tulips? Rows of tiny jade-green beads that hung like weeping willow branches to her shoulders? Or a delicate pair made of wires twisted into the shape of tiny roses? How did one pick earrings fancy enough to ensnare a husband?

She had settled on the green beads. The roses were more suited to Louise, and one of Mandy's workmates would love the red glo-mesh and had offered to pay a hundred dollars cash for anything Jodie could promise was a one-off. Decision made!

'Thanks,' she said, her voice sounding as though

she'd just smoked a packet of cigarettes. 'I make them myself. My styles are based on flowers I used to find at the Chelsea Gardens as a little girl.'

Shut-up, Jodie! He said he liked them, not that he wanted to buy a pair. But he liked them? Oh, no, he wasn't…was he? She'd already met one of those the night before. And that was all well and good, but if *this* man was permanently unavailable to all women, that would be a nasty cosmic joke.

'They're…nice,' he said, sticking out his bottom lip and nodding.

And in a blinding flash of relief Jodie realised *he* was being *nice*. If he'd said her earrings were *fabulous* she ought to have been worried. But nice? That just meant Heath was a guy paying a girl a compliment.

'Now tell me about your work,' she said, wholeheartedly moving on. Jodie was simply not used to talking about herself. She didn't even really know enough about herself to be sure what she said was the truth. 'I gather you are some sort of cowboy, throwing hay bales and milking cows all day?'

Cowboy? Where had that come from? Even she heard the note of flirtation in her voice and so it wasn't such a shock when his blue eyes glittered.

'So who's looking after your cows while you're away?' she asked, keeping her voice neat and even.

He ran a lean hand beneath his mouth. Then he looked up at her from beneath a sweep of thick chestnut eyelashes, which were superior to hers even with the modern marvel of long-lash mascara at her disposal. 'I have a station manager, Andy, who runs the place in my absence, as well as numerous seasonal staff who do most of the heavy labour. So apart from throwing hay bales about the place, I am also a qualified civil engineer.'

Oh! So maybe the whole 'outback farmer' thing had just been a means to an introduction, a hook, a way to get a girl interested. Maybe he lived in town in a nice big house big enough for her and Louise and for Lisa and Mandy to crash after a girls' night out...

'Do you get much of a chance to engineer anything civilly while out on the farm?'

'Some. A little. I've completely redesigned the irrigation system at Jamesons Run and rigged up a lever-and-pulley system to help in the barn, so, yeah, I like to keep my hand in. But wrangling cattle is pretty much a full-time gig nowadays,' Heath said, leaning his chin on his palm as he gazed at her.

Oh. Well, that answered that one. He talked like a city boy. He walked like a city boy. He even had a city-boy degree. But he was a farmer. With a farm. Damn it!

Because it was clear he wasn't running from the idea of being a husband in a hurry. *Her* husband in a hurry. Though neither of them had mentioned it in so many words, they both knew why they were there. And after having met one another, they were both…still…there…

'I take it you've never wrangled cattle before,' he said.

'Not lately,' she said, the idea of doing such a thing petrifying her to the soles of her feet.

'When reading your bio, I figured as much.' He leaned forward, until their faces were so close that she could see perfect midnight-blue rings around his irises. 'Yet I still came tonight, and so did you.'

'I guess that means neither of us are entirely sensible,' she agreed, her voice dropping to accommodate their close proximity. 'About what we want.'

'To us,' he said, tipping his bottle her way before taking another swig. 'And to not being sensible.'

Jodie felt warm and fuzzy, as if she were having some sort of out-of-body experience. Maybe it was the wine. Maybe it was the excess of bread yeast in her system. Maybe it was the company.

As she found herself fast becoming lost in

Heath's heavenly eyes, something caught Jodie's attention. Mandy was waving a frantic arm at her, poking a manic finger at her wrist-watch. It seemed her next date was already there.

But Jodie wasn't yet ready for this to end.

'Look,' she said, leaning in, feeling more terrified and more brave and less sensible than she had in a long time, 'I'll be honest with you. There is another prospect waiting for me at the bar, but I've been here so many times in the past few nights I feel as though my bottom is changing shape to match this chair. Do you want to get out of here?'

Heath's warm blue eyes blinked. Narrowed. And then lit from within as he got her meaning. 'I don't know. I'm in the mood for something lathered in chocolate. Does this place serve good desserts?'

Jodie shook her head. 'I wouldn't know. I never eat sweets.'

He was a cowboy; she was a city girl. He wanted chocolate; she hadn't eaten chocolate in a decade. What the heck was she playing at? By the look in his eyes she wondered if he was thinking exactly the same thing.

But then something shifted. Before she was able to identify what, he looked at his watch—silver, sturdy, knocked-about—and said, 'Well, then, it seems we have to find another place in which to continue this conversation. I don't have to head back home until tomorrow afternoon, so for the next fifteen hours I'm all yours.'

All hers. Her heart did a neat little flip inside her chest. And heart flips were bad.

She tore her confounded gaze away from Heath to find Lisa had joined in the frantic waving. It seemed there were now two guys awaiting her. But if she had to say the words, 'So tell me about your job,' one more time…

Jodie stood, and with shaking hands patted her napkin against her mouth. 'Meet me at the street crossing on the city side of the building,' she murmured. 'Five minutes.'

Heath looked up at her with more than mischief in his bright blue eyes. 'Shall do, Ms Bond.'

Jodie turned and, without looking back, headed for the ladies' room where she had a date with a tiny window and a Dumpster.

Heath turned on his chair and watched Jodie walk away, keeping a close eye on the tidy package within the hipster jeans, the bouncy auburn hair, and the expanse of creamy skin exposed by her glittery contraption of a top that was held together by modern-day engineering and luck.

He blew out a long slow breath when she finally sauntered from view.

In her website picture she had been worth a

second glance, but in the flesh those intense green eyes of hers were just something else—relentless yet radiating unexpected vulnerability. He'd had to stop himself time and again from reaching out and running a soothing finger over her furrowed brow as every worry that had run through her mind had flashed across her eyes like a freeway warning sign.

One of those flashing signals had told him what she saw of him she liked, and, even without all the other inducements she offered, that was a pretty potent thing to find in a first date. And a blind date at that.

So while half of him couldn't quite believe that he was with a woman whose intention to marry wasn't just a niggling presumption in the back of his head, but a blatant prerequisite to his spending time with her, the other half of him found that the most heady inducement of all.

Added to that there was something about being with a city girl that took him away from his troubles back home. Something about the powders and potions they used to look after themselves. They always smelled so good. He wondered if he would get close enough to Jodie that night to find if she smelled half as good as he imagined she would.

And Jodie was not only a city girl, but a

foreign city girl to boot. A girl with skin so creamy it was never meant to be exposed to the harsh Australian clime, with hair so fine it gleamed, and with an accent so strong that every word she uttered reminded him that there was a big world out there that he had been ignoring for the longest time. Until now.

Heath looked towards the front door where the blonde who had shown him to his table stood fighting with a rangy brunette. Both were staring at the ladies' room door. Jodie's last line of defence, perhaps?

The brunette glanced over at his table and he gave her a small wave. She grabbed the blonde and ducked behind her, leaving the blonde having to wave back. Yep. They both belonged to Jodie for sure. City girls and their mates...

With a secret smile, he turned back to his beer, his mind whirling through the night so far. But then he groaned as he remembered blurting out, 'I am also a qualified civil engineer.'

How long had it been since he had even said those words out loud? Sure, they were true—he would have been eminently employable in the field if not for the fateful timing that had forced him to return to his outback home to look after his younger brothers and sisters and to run the family farm.

But why had he needed to let this slip of a girl

know such information? Because she had been so obviously trying to reconcile to herself what the heck she was doing sitting across a table from a *farmer*, that was why! Well, he was more than that, just as he was sure that behind those liquid eyes there was more light and shade to Jodie Simpson than she was letting through her shield as well.

Thinking of light, he could still remember the radiance in Cameron's eyes the day he had married Marissa. He remembered the scent of roses from Marissa's bouquet as he had hugged her after the ceremony. She had thanked him that day, for being a good friend, to her and especially to Cameron.

The picture dissolved as he remembered the darkness in Cameron's eyes as he'd sat in the funeral chapel while his young wife's coffin had lain quiet and sombre to his right. The depth of Cameron's sorrow rocked Heath to his very soul.

In his brother Heath had witnessed the extremes of both bliss and despair. But at thirty-six years of age he had never known either firsthand. His life had been lived by the rules and where had that put him? Alone.

Light and shade. It was way past time his stagnant life was injected with more of both. This was a woman who could take him out of his comfort zone. Jodie was a woman who wanted change so badly she was willing to risk everything by marrying a complete stranger in order to get it. Nothing ventured, nothing gained, right?

He pushed back his chair and walked towards the front door and the two women all but fell over themselves to look natural.

He reached into his pocket and pulled out his wallet.

'Is everything all right?' the blonde asked.

'It's fine, apart from the fact that my...date seems to have left me with the bill.' He gave her enough money to more than cover his one beer and Jodie's untouched glass of wine.

Then, with a spring in his step that would have been more appropriate for an eighteen-year-old buck on the prowl rather than someone twice that age, he stuck his hands in his trouser pockets and stepped out into a mild spring darkness feeling like a car whose battery had been jump-started after being flat for a decade.

CHAPTER THREE

SUNDAY morning Jodie pushed back the comforter, hitched up her too-loose flannelette pyjama pants, and yawned magnificently as she opened her bedroom door.

Louise, already showered and dressed in what amounted to a casual outfit for her—a lemon twin set and designer jeans—turned on the couch with a hand to her throat. 'Oh, my. I thought I was the only one here.'

'Mandy and Lisa have gone out?' Jodie asked.

Louise nodded. Jodie looked to the clock on the microwave to find it was only nine in the morning. They'd still not been home when Jodie had snuck in at three that morning, so they would have had five hours' sleep at the most.

Jodie shuffled to the couch on which Louise had slept, though you wouldn't know it by the neat throw rug over the back of the chair and the perfectly placed scatter cushions. Louise sat, crossing her feet neatly at the ankle, an open bucket of ice cream before her. Jodie sat on her hand to stop herself from mussing up her sister's perfect hair.

'What's with the nine in the morning ice-cream fix?' Jodie asked.

Louise offered her spoon, but Jodie declined.

'Mum…Ivy…just called.' Poor Louise's face crumpled as she fought to settle on how she ought to think of the woman who had brought her up as her own. 'But that's neither here nor there. Tell me about your night. Did you meet anyone brilliant?'

Jodie wasn't quite sure what to say. While her life felt as if it was on the up and up, Louise's was falling apart at her feet.

Before searching out Jodie, Louise had discovered that before she was born her father had sired illegitimate twin sons. And they were back, wanting to take their place in the infamous Valentine family. The shock had sent her father into cardiac arrest, and, believing he was dying, he had told her that she was adopted. Shattered to find herself the object of so many lies, she had registered to find her birth mother and, in discovering Patricia was uncontactable, she had found Jodie instead and flown to Australia in an instant. Now Jodie was Louise's only support—the only person in her life not in any way linked to her complicated adoptive family.

'It went okay,' Jodie said, playing down mightily how much better than okay her night with Heath Jameson had been. After escaping The Cave, she and Heath had walked for hours, following their feet up boulevards and down side streets, as they'd enjoyed the balmy spring night.

And they had talked. The subject of Jodie's disinclination for and Heath's love of chocolate had kept them going for an hour all on its own. They had never even found the dessert Heath had been hankering for; instead, hours later they had settled for a kebab when a take-away van had loomed in their meandering path.

'Come on, Lou, what happened with Ivy? Tell me.'

Louise half nodded and half shook her head. 'It was awkward to say the least. I thought I would be upset, or angry. But I just felt numb.'

'Did you talk to your dad?'

Louise shook her head. 'I'm livid enough at her, but I'm nowhere near ready to tackle the mistrust I feel for him. He didn't just lie to me; he lied to so many of us. If I didn't have you here, now, and this place…'

Jodie leant over and gave Louise a one-armed squeeze. 'I'm glad you're here too,' Jodie said. 'Truly. And stay as long as you like. No worries. You might even fall in love with the place as I have.'

Louise smiled at her, her blue-grey eyes so familiar. So much like Patricia's. For one blinding moment, Jodie missed her mum, and wondered where she was. She hadn't heard from her in a few weeks since she and her new husband Derek had started travelling, but if they hit trouble surely he would let her know and ask her to come home and…

No. That wasn't her place now.

'No worries?' Louise repeated. 'There was a definite Australian accent there.'

'Really?' Jodie liked that idea very much.

'Absolutely. And you've got the whole relaxed Aussie thing going on as well. I'm wondering if it comes to you all through the sun rays.'

Jodie laughed. 'I think it must. Back home I was a right Londoner. Cool, grey, and with all the vigour of a wet winter's day.'

Jodie's mind shot once again to her night with Heath. He was the perfect embodiment of all the things she loved about Australia—warmth, ease, leisure—the antithesis of bleak, wet, bustling London. Was that why she had been so instantly drawn to him? So ready to know him outside the loaded atmosphere of The Cave, to pretend that it was a real date?

Louise sighed. 'Listening to you talk with your lovely half-Australian accent, home seems so far away it almost feels unreal.'

Jodie knew just what she meant. She loved the fact that her life here felt unreal. Unreality was bliss. Jodie reached out and took her by the hand. 'Do you understand now why I have to do whatever I can to stay?'

Louise's cool blue-grey eyes filled with an even mix of sadness and understanding. She sighed and Jodie knew everything between them was going to be okay. 'I am actually a little jealous of you, you know. I wish I was in your shoes, with my future a blank canvas before me. Nothing tying me down. Nothing drawing me home.'

'But you are. You are just like me. Simply choose to stay. For real. Stay for ever.'

A ray of sun seemed to break through the dark cloud hanging over Louise's head. 'Ha! Wouldn't that shock the pants off the whole lot of them? Max, my cousin, would have a conniption fit if he heard that I, the perennial good girl, ran away from home never to return. Well, I guess he's not really my cousin now, if you come to think about it. But, oh, I would still love to see the look on his face—'

A noise at the front door called their attention. Mandy and Lisa spilled inside carrying their regular Sunday-morning French sticks and Brie.

'Well, well, well. Look what the cat dragged in,' Mandy said as she threw the brown paper bags onto the counter. 'When you didn't come back out of the bathroom last night, we thought you had fallen in. You took off with the hot farmer, didn't you?'

'Well, actually yes, I did,' Jodie said, glancing at Louise, who had managed to drag herself away from her deep dark thoughts about her non-cousin Max and was now watching her with renewed interest.

'Now, Jodie, you made no mention of a hot farmer.' By the smile in her eyes Jodie knew that her understanding outweighed her sadness. Jodie could have hugged her.

'I had to tell the others you'd fallen ill,' Lisa said, not nearly as impressed with Jodie's antics as Mandy. 'With megalomania. And since none of them even knew what the word meant we figured you had made the right decision to leave. So, when's the big day?'

Jodie flapped a hand at her unmoved friend. 'Don't be silly. Heath is the last one I would choose.'

Mandy stopped with a hunk of cheese halfway to her mouth and Jodie knew she had laid it on too thick.

'Okay, maybe not the last one. Scott from across the hall would beat him to that title by a whisker.'

'Time is marching on. And if hot farm boy is only good for a one-night-on-the-town fling,'

Mandy said, 'who the heck *is* going to be the lucky Mr Jodie Simpson?'

Jodie struggled to remember any of the candidates she had met before Heath had walked in the door, but they were mostly a blur.

It didn't help that she still felt Heath all around her. The scent of his aftershave lingered on her hair as the night before he had used her wrap as a prop when he'd been doing an impersonation of one of his four sisters. She could still taste sweet chilli sauce on her tongue from the kebab they had shared. And every time she closed her eyes, she could see Heath's crinkly eyes and smiling, tanned face imprinted there.

'Umm, maybe Barnaby, the visual merchandiser,' she said, plucking a name from the furthest recesses of her mind. 'He would be willing to marry me for rent-free accommodation here. Apparently his favourite gay bar is just around the corner.'

'So why didn't you run away with him?' Louise asked, and Jodie no longer felt like hugging her clever sister.

Mandy grinned at Louise. 'She makes a good point.'

'I…I'd had enough by the time Heath came along. If I had to ask one more guy to tell me about himself, I was going to drown myself in a whole bottle of red wine.'

'Oh, balderdash,' Lisa said. 'You fell over when I brought Heath to your table, Jodes.'

'My foot had fallen asleep,' she argued.

'Please! No part of a woman's body could possibly sleep through that. He was gorgeous.' This time Lisa got the full-stare treatment from all three girls. 'Well, he was.'

Jodie raked both hands through her hair. 'Okay. Fine. He was gorgeous. But he comes from a family of seven. After growing up in the middle of London with my crazy mother my only known relative, I've only just discovered I have a half-sister.'

Jodie glanced at Louise, who smiled warmly back. Okay, so hugging was back on the family agenda.

'Besides which,' Jodie continued, 'he lives on a farm, and I live here. And I want to stay here. And he wants…' She wasn't really sure what he wanted. They had never really discussed it; they had both had too much of a nice time specifically not talking specifics.

'What does he want?' Lisa asked.

'What he *deserves* is the real deal.'

Mandy shook her head in utter confusion, while Lisa looked at her with too much understanding for Jodie's comfort.

'So what next?' Lisa asked, kindly pinning the

attention elsewhere. 'Do we tell Barnaby the gay visual merchandiser the happy news?'

Somehow Jodie couldn't rouse any excitement for the idea. 'Maybe not just yet.'

'Right. That's the spirit!' Mandy ran to the desk in the corner and clicked on the Internet connection. 'Let's first see what new men the night has brought us.'

Though it was the last thing she wanted to do, Jodie moved to look over Mandy's shoulder. And, oh, what choices she had! A lawyer with three teenaged children, a baker looking for a morning person, and a guy who had been on the dole for eight years while he ran a campaign to legalise marijuana in his 'spare time'.

Time was running out. The calendar above the computer with its bright red crosses showed how little time she did have until The Day She Had To Leave. That decided it for her—she would choose by the end of that day.

Barnaby, Scott, or Heath.

For Heath was still on the maybe list whether she admitted it to the girls or not.

After driving her home the night before, he had walked her to the front door of her apartment building. Shadows and moonlight had slanted across his strong face as they had stood facing one another beneath the ivy-trellised alcove. Her skin still tingled from the feel of his smooth cheek against hers as he had kissed her goodnight.

'Can I see you again?' he had asked, his deep voice washing over her.

Jodie's cheeks flushed pink as she remembered the moment the romantic young girl she had once been before life had beaten her down, the young girl who had spent many a night wishing on the first star, had risen up and answered him with, 'I would like that.'

The phone rang and, saved by the bell, Jodie leapt for it so fast the phone flew out of her hand. It took some world-class juggling to make sure it didn't fall.

'Who-yello!' she said when she pulled it to her ear.

'Jodie.'

She knew that voice in an instant. Heath. The deep vibrations tickled through her hand, down her arm and into her stomach.

'Oh,' she gasped. 'Hi. Hang on a sec, will you?'

She shoved a hand over the mouthpiece and climbed over the back of the couch. 'It's for me. I'll take it while I'm having a bath. Two birds with one stone and all that. So save me some Brie. Right? Okay.'

She ran into the bathroom, cringing at the mixed looks of bewilderment and perception on her friends' faces.

'Heath. I'm back,' she said once she had closed the door and heard the girls' voices start up in conversation.

'And bathing, I hear.'

'Oh, no,' she said, feeling her cheeks pink. 'Not yet. Fully clothed over here.'

'Pity,' he said, taking his time to let the word go.

'I wasn't expecting to hear from you again. So soon,' she added belatedly.

'Well, I do have to be home again in four hours,' Heath said, 'so I thought it best to spend my short time here wisely. Asking you to have morning tea with me feels like the wisest move I've made in a long time. A kind of reciprocation for the two-a.m. kebab.'

To block out her conversation, Jodie sat on the edge of the bath and turned on the old taps before pouring in excessive amounts of strawberry bath bubbles. She breathed in deep through her nose as she tried to decide what to do.

On the up side, she and Heath got on well. Ridiculously well. And that was important. What use would it be wasting two years of her life living with someone who drove her around the bend?

But on the down side, Heath Jameson was also charming and way too attractive for comfort. And for that exact reason she ought *not* to take it any further. She wanted a two-year husband, not a boyfriend. These next two years would be instrumental in her continued self-discovery, and she could not possibly achieve that if her time was spent with someone to whom she felt connected. For Jodie was a woman who had never learnt how to sever connections, no matter how self-destructive they might be.

'So?' he finally asked when she had stalled too long. 'Are you up for it? Has the kebab digested enough that it's time for a refill?'

Jodie slid her back further down the wall until her knees were level with her nose. Her stomach did feel empty, hollow, and tingling, but that was only half the reason she gave in and said, 'Yeah, I'm up for it.'

She gave in because she had to let him off the hook face to face. He was worthy of that.

'Great. I'll pick you up in fifteen,' he said.

He was gone before Jodie had the chance to explain to him that she would meet him downstairs. There was no way she was going to let the girls know that she was seeing him again. It was bad enough that she knew that she was fast becoming enchanted by the guy. If they had any inkling, they might just try to talk her out of letting him go.

* * *

Fourteen minutes later, bathed and dressed in track pants, a white T-shirt and sneakers, Jodie sidled out into the kitchen.

'Brunch is ready,' Louise said, waving a French stick and a round of Brie at her.

'Not for me.' She placed the phone casually back on the cradle.

Lisa took one look at her garb and lifted two shocked eyebrows. 'Going *jogging*, are we?'

'A walk, at least. I'm feeling the need to exercise away all those bread rolls and red wine I've ingested over the last two weeks.'

'Bread doesn't make you fat,' Mandy insisted, biting down onto a piece of bread smothered in soft cheese. 'It's all in your head. Think thin and you'll be thin. Jogging is for suckers.'

They all turned to glare at naturally stick-thin Mandy who had no idea how good she had it.

'Well, this sucker will be back in a while.' With a quick wave over her shoulder, Jodie slipped out the door and ran down the three flights of stairs just as Heath reached the front alcove where they had said their moonlight goodbyes only hours before.

'Hi! Don't! I'm here!' she cried out, so that he wouldn't reach for the doorbell. The poor guy flinched.

'So you are,' he said. 'And all in a rush to see me.'

Jodie opened her mouth to negate that idea, but then realised it was probably easier to let it lie. 'Hungry, remember?' she said.

Tugging a cute pink cardigan over her T-shirt to dress up her outfit just a tad, she took the opportunity to find out if he really was as attractive as she had remembered him. Lo and behold, in the harsh light of day, Heath Jameson—in chinos and blue and cream Hawaiian shirt that set off his eyes, his tan, and his general gorgeousness beautifully—was pure masculine heaven. Ouch!

'Ready?' he asked, and then he smiled, his face coming over all warm and encouraging, and Jodie had to abstain from leaning against him just to soak up some of that Australian warmth that Louise had begun to notice in her.

'So, where are you taking me?' she asked.

'To heights of gastronomic pleasure the likes of which you have never seen.'

Heath drove from Jodie's apartment back towards his beachside St Kilda hotel, stealing glances at the woman in the passenger seat of his car.

He had spent a good portion of his morning wondering if his great first impression of Jodie had been falsely remembered. In the light of their secret tryst out into the Melbourne night, her side-splitting tales of her time at the hands of her meddling housemates, and with the addition of a truly fantastic kebab to finish off the night, he thought perhaps he had been so hoping for it to be perfect that he had indeed willed it to be the best blind date any guy had ever known.

But as Jodie had leapt through the doorway like a whirlwind of nervous energy just now, madly pulling her auburn waves into a quick pony-tail, flapping that bright pink cardigan at him like a flag at a bull, her wide green eyes wild with panic as he reached for the doorbell—obviously because she didn't want her roommates to know what she was up to—he knew his concerns had been unfounded.

She was bright. Complicated. Nervous as an unbroken colt. Utterly lovely. And she smelled so good he had to remind himself to breathe out as well as in.

Last night he hadn't been able to put his finger on it, some lingering sweetness that played with his senses. But this morning it came to him like the subtle scent of grass after a storm. Strawberries.

As he pulled his car into a park on the St Kilda Esplanade, just near a row of white-sailed market stalls, he shot a look her way.

Something in her demeanour had him thinking she was preparing to give him the brush-off, but he wasn't having any of it. He was struck by her.

Truly struck. And a risk was not a risk if the path to your goal was clear.

And since he didn't believe a word of her claim that she hated desserts as much as she said she did, he took her to the one place in Melbourne that would tempt her to change her mind.

If anything could.

CHAPTER FOUR

WITHIN minutes, the French pastry shops on Acland Street in St Kilda loomed. Jodie had heard rumours of such a place and had quite purposely never been down this road.

Ten-foot-high windows each showcased a dozen shelves packed with melting moments, glimmering fruit tarts, decadent éclairs and every sweet delight a person could crave. Like someone trapped in the desert for ten years, Jodie was drawn towards the mirage, her tastebuds going into overdrive as long-ago memories tickled at her senses.

The feel of pastry melting on her tongue. Sherbet crackling against her lips. And chocolate. Oh, the heavenly melting sensation that was chocolate.

The truth was, Jodie loved desserts, but her mother was diabetic, and corruptibly so. Patricia was so lacking in will-power Jodie had once found her passed out on the kitchen table with an empty bottle of chocolate syrup beside her. Since that day, Jodie had doggedly trained herself to live without the taste of sugar.

'Come on, order something sweet,' Heath offered. 'Anything you like. It's on me.'

Jodie perused the glassed-in rows of cakes and was stoic. Even though Patricia was nowhere in sight, it was a testament to her own continuing will-power, her very difference from her imprudent mother, that she do without.

'Tea, black, no sugar, and a savoury scroll.'

'Come on! This place is the Mecca for dessert lovers. It's legendary. You can't possibly be telling me that there is *nothing* sweet here that can tempt you.'

Oh, yeah. There sure was. Which was why she was being a good strong girl and ordering something not decadent in the least. 'Sorry. I am a tea and scroll kind of girl.'

His eyes narrowed and she realised her words had held a tinge of bitterness she had not meant to reveal. She smiled inanely and moved inside to the counter where she placed her order.

'Add two chocolate croissants and a tall black to the order. Three sugars and a small jug of milk on the side. Ta,' Heath said from somewhere behind her, his breath washing over the back of her hair. 'Don't panic, both croissants are for me. One's for the road.'

He reached around her with a twenty-dollar note and Jodie moved ever so slightly to avoid the brush of his arm against hers. But she wasn't quick enough to avoid the divine feel of his hand against her back as he led her to a table outside.

'So when do you have to be home?' she asked. *Tell me you have to go in five minutes and I will be so very very thankful!*

He didn't even look at his battered watch. 'Before dark. I have cattle going to market tomorrow and so tonight will be my last chance to inspect them.'

She nodded, though she hadn't a clue what he had just said. She had been too focussed on the crooked smile that lay about his mouth with such ease. Her will-power had kept her from chocolate, pastries, and whipped cream for nigh on ten years. She had done without sugar. She could do without him. And it was past time to let him know.

'Heath.' Her voice quavered, so she coughed discreetly into her closed fist.

'Ye-es,' he said, his voice low and deep as though he knew her next words would be weighty.

'I know we didn't exactly hit on this last night, but I just wanted to make sure we were on the same page. I did not meet with you last night, looking for a date, but for a husband in a hurry, as it were.'

He blinked. Once. Twice. Then he leant his chin on his fist. 'Right,' he said, waiting for her to go on.

'So, why are you still here?'

Though she ached to look away, at the ceiling, at her fingernails, anywhere but at those bright blue eyes, she didn't. It felt like one of those moments in life, like when you get your final exam results at the end of school, or when your mum tells you that the man who brought you up until he left in the middle of the night when you were thirteen years old might not even be your father. It was one of those clincher moments that changed everything before and everything to come depending on the answer.

'I came because a couple of weeks ago an old…friend of mine died,' he finally said. 'Her name was Marissa.'

Jodie's breath locked in her lungs. Of all the reasons she could have imagined, that would not have been one of them.

Heath flaked pieces of pastry from his croissant and laid them in a neat pile on his plate as he spoke. 'We knew one another in college. Several years later she married my brother Cameron. They had to overcome a fair bit of flak to be together, but we all came to see that they were made for one another.'

Jodie could hear the care he was taking in choosing his words, and she knew he was holding back. Pain? Details? Something deeper?

'What happened?' she asked, her voice husky as she absorbed the unexpected emotion unwinding from within this seemingly perfectly content man. Maybe he wasn't so content after all. Maybe he had met with her as he was searching for some way to fix his life too.

'Two and a half weeks ago Marissa was in her station wagon, on her way to pick up the kids from day-care, when she was sideswiped by a guy running a red light.'

Jodie reached out to lay a hand over Heath's but pulled away at the last second when she saw how white his knuckles had become. He noticed, and a small grimace crossed his face.

'I realised at that moment that I had never even come close to having what they had,' Heath continued. 'And it felt like I was copping out by not trying to find out if I even could. Marissa and Cameron showed me that the greatest rewards in life only come from taking the greatest risks. And I decided it's time I take the leap.'

Jodie knew how that felt. It felt as if she were standing on a precipice, looking out to the horizon, not sure if her next step would land on solid ground or slip away beneath her for ever.

Leaping would sure solve that tension. The bite of savoury scroll suddenly tasted bitter in Jodie's mouth. So much so, she had to reach up with her paper napkin and casually remove the lump.

He looked back at her, his blue eyes dark and intense. 'I am past the age of finding myself another college sweetheart. Working on a cattle station I'm surrounded by men day in and day out and I don't have the luxury of dating around, finding a woman I like, and wooing her. But now I don't have to worry about all that.'

Jodie knew he was saying he no longer needed to look, as he had found her. Her untried heart did a somersault in her chest. She slapped it down. He wasn't saying that he fancied her. He was only saying that marriage was the biggest risk he could think to take. But what was he risking? His heart? Doubtful. His fortune? Ha! He was a farmer, for goodness' sake. Maybe it was a mid-life crisis and he was merely looking for a way to shake things up in his life. Well, she sure was no angel to live with so if that was the case he would get a shake-up beyond his wildest dreams.

But no. No. No! Just because she might be exactly what he was looking for didn't mean that the reverse was true. In that moment she wished Heath were a eunuch. A eunuch with Heath's kindness but maybe a little less charm, buck teeth, a lisp, hair sprouting from his ears, decidedly non-blue eyes, a nice big house around the corner from her apartment, and he spent more time away on business than he did at home. As this way she would have found her man. Someone nice, unassuming and unaffecting with whom to share a home and a marriage certificate for the next two years.

But he was so clearly none of those things. He was completely affecting, so affecting she forgot herself around him, and the whole point of this exercise was not to forget herself, but to find herself. So she had no choice but to disentangle this fish from her net and let him go.

'You have your own reasons to want to marry,' he said into the growing silence. 'I am thinking visa issues?'

Jodie nodded.

'How long do you have?'

'Fifty-four days,' Jodie said without even having to think about it. 'I have time.' *Not much, but enough.*

He blinked up at her, holding her gaze effortlessly. 'Being a consummate Aussie bloke, I haven't had much practice at this sort of thing, but what I am trying to say, badly I'm sure, is that you don't need time. I am healthy. I am an Australian citizen. I am financially independent. I have no diseases. I like you and I think you like me too.

And I think that liking one another is a pretty good base from which to launch a life together.'

Diseases? What the heck did diseases have to do with it unless…? Oh. Jodie swallowed hard before she became for ever lost in the sort of life together Heath was imagining.

'Heath, I'm afraid that you have me all wrong. I apologise for not clearing this all up sooner.' *Before you liked me, and before I felt this potent attraction to so very many things about you.*

'My plan is to marry so that in two years' time I will end up with a Permanent Visa. That is the end point for me. Then the man I have married and I will split. Divorce. Go our separate ways.'

He watched her, his expression unchanging, so that she had no idea what was going on behind those bottomless blue eyes.

'I can't give anyone the promise of a proper life together, whether he and I like each other or not,' she said. 'I just can't. And at this point in my life, I don't want to. I know I'm asking a lot, but I have to be strong about this—two years is all I intend to give.'

'May I ask why you feel you need an end point?' Heath asked.

Okay. So she owed him that much at least. 'I've been in a…relationship with someone for several years whereby I was in charge of every facet of their life. Without me to look out for their every whim, craving, and concern, they would not have survived. That is a responsibility I do not wish to take on again. I realise that may sound selfish but—'

'No,' he said. 'I see your point.' And though she expected to see a cold, hard flint in his eye at the extent of her selfishness, there was none. But she felt there was a 'but' coming, and she wasn't wrong.

'But I don't need someone to look out for my every whim, craving or concern, Jodie. I'm a big boy and I've been doing all that for myself for more years than I can count.'

The more he spoke, the more she sank deeper and deeper into those eyes, and into a wish to believe that he was right and she was wrong.

Why hadn't she met him some other time? A year before. Five years before. Why couldn't he have been some London guy who one day when she was out getting groceries came along and swept her off her feet, giving her a ray of sunshine in her hard grey life back home?

But no. Everything about him was so Australian. He would wilt in such a place as London. Or perhaps he would stand out all the more, a beacon of warmth that women would flock to. Back in London she would not have stood a chance with such a guy.

But now? Here? The fates had decreed that if

she wanted him, she could have him. As a two-year husband. Acquaintances only? No way. She wasn't sure she could trust herself to keep such a deal much less enforce such rules upon him. If that was what she wanted she should never have looked past Barnaby the visual merchandiser. So no. Heath Jameson, lovely and charming and gorgeous as he was, was now officially off the list.

Ready to tell him exactly that, Jodie started when her mobile phone buzzed and beeped at her hip. With an apologetic glance at Heath, she checked to find a message from Lisa.

'Come home. Quick. Lou's had bad news.'

Jodie was on her feet in a heartbeat. 'I have to go. Now.'

Heath tucked his napkin beneath his plate and joined her on his feet. 'What's happened?'

'I'm not sure. But something's wrong with my sister.'

She looked up the teeming sidewalk, realising it was a long walk back to her apartment. When she looked back at Heath, he was already moving around the table to herd her along.

'Come on. I'll drive you home.'

After the endless drive in which Jodie had not been able to get through to Louise's mobile, or the home phone, she leapt from the car before it had barely stopped.

She shot a quick, 'Thanks,' over her shoulder to Heath before unlocking the front door, shooting up three flights of stairs and barging into the apartment where she found Lisa whispering into the cordless phone, Mandy sitting on the couch, wringing her hands and not quite knowing where to look, while Louise sat at the hall table with her luggage packed beside her.

Louise's face was pale and her eyes puffy. All of Jodie's carer instincts flooded to the fore and she slid to her knees in front of her sister, feeling her temperature, taking her pulse, and checking her eyes for a response before she even realised she had been doing so.

'What's going on?' Jodie asked, moving her fretting hands to take hold of Louise's cold fists.

'Just after you left I had an awful call from my dad.'

'Is it another heart attack? Is he okay?'

Louise shook her head. 'No. Nothing like that. But the money's gone. All of it.'

Jodie fought hard to keep up. 'What money?'

'Dad went to pay a tax bill and found the restaurant account empty. Someone's taken it. Stephanie, the manager of the Bella Lucia at Knightsbridge, would normally help look after such things but she has had to go back to America urgently. I'm all he has.'

Lisa hung up the phone, the beep ringing loud in the heavy air. 'I've organised a car and driver to pick you up when you get to Heathrow, Lou.'

Louise nodded her thanks.

Heathrow? Oh, no, not Heathrow.

'Surely there is someone else. Someone already there.' Jodie frantically searched for a name Louise had mentioned. Anybody else who could help so Louise didn't have to leave her so soon.

'What about Max?' Louise had talked a lot about her cousin Max, though more often in derision than devotion.

Louise shook her head and Jodie saw the glitter of diamond-bright tears in her pale grey eyes. 'Dad would never go to Max. The reasons are complicated.'

Jodie heard the front door close softly.

Lisa's face turned to stone, while Mandy's mouth dropped open in surprise. Jodie didn't have to look over her shoulder to know that Heath was in the doorway. But she did anyway.

He took one look at her, then headed straight for the kitchen. Jodie heard cupboards open and close and the tap go on, then off, and then Heath was there with a glass of water. He gave it to her, and she gave it to Louise.

Louise had a sip, then let the glass loll to the side and Heath reached out to catch it. Louise barely noticed. Her eyes were glazed and far away and Jodie could feel herself losing the battle.

Her eyes finally focussed on Jodie. 'Thank you so much for having me, Jodie. I can't tell you how much I have needed this and you. But now it's time to go home. They've booked me a flight that leaves this afternoon. Dad…my dad needs me.'

But I need you, Jodie wanted to scream.

She had never felt so much as if she needed someone in her life. Knowing that her mother wasn't her only blood tie in the world, and knowing that Louise was sane, and sensible, and well adjusted, gave her hope that genetically she had such a chance as well. Now that Louise was going away, Jodie suddenly felt weak and frightened and alone.

But Jodie also knew how hard it was for a child to say no to such a plea from a parent, no matter how fraught the relationship.

Suddenly feeling as if the precipice she had been balancing on had finally dropped away from beneath her knees, Jodie blurted out, 'I'll come with you.'

Out of the corner of her eye she saw Mandy move before Lisa's hand clamped down on her shoulder keeping her in place.

'My return ticket is open-ended,' Jodie continued. 'Give me an hour to pack, and call the airline, and I'll come back home with you.'

Louise snapped out of her trance and shot a glance over Jodie's shoulder and Jodie remembered Heath was still there. 'No,' Lou said, her voice now firm, 'you won't.'

Jodie shot a frustrated glance at Heath to find him leaning against the entryway wall watching her, his expression careful. She could see he was clinging to every word she was saying. But she couldn't deal with that now. He would have to get in line.

'My visa's about to run out anyway,' Jodie said, focussing fully on Louise. 'Maybe it's a sign. There's so much more I want to know, and say…'

Louise pulled Jodie into her slim arms. 'We have years to get to all that. But right now you have the chance to stay in this fabulous part of the world. If I was in your shoes I would focus on that goal with all my might. I, on the other hand, have too much unfinished business at home. We'll see each other again. There or here. I look forward to the day we can get together, you, Patricia and me.'

The thought of her mum's reaction to Louise showing up frightened Jodie to bits. Would Patricia fall apart and need Jodie to pick her up again as she had a hundred times before when things had become too hard? But at the same time the idea of the three of them sitting down to lunch was so like a dream come true it physically hurt.

'Promise?' Jodie said, fighting to stave back tears now herself.

'With all my heart.'

No longer able to feel her limbs, Jodie struggled to stand. 'You at least have to let me drive you to the airport.'

'No,' Heath said, his deep voice catching them all unawares. 'Please allow me.'

'Thanks, but no,' Jodie shot at him.

'You pointed out your car to me last night, remember,' he said, his expression showing he didn't believe Rusty would get around the block, much less to the airport.

Jodie bristled, ready to tell the guy exactly where he could put his car when Heath reached down and took a hold of Louise's heavy designer luggage as though it were light grocery bags.

'If we take my car,' he said, 'you guys can sit in the back and talk on the way.'

Heath smiled, and Jodie's breaking heart clenched with such fierce and sudden attraction she wasn't sure it knew what it was thinking. She took two deep breaths, then nodded. 'That would be much appreciated.'

When Lisa finally let her off her leash, Mandy ran to Louise, wrapping her in a tight hug. 'We'll miss you, Lou. Come back and stay with us any time.'

Lisa moved in more slowly and gave her a quick kiss on the cheek. 'Our door is always open.'

'Thank you, guys,' Louise said, 'so very much.'

'Come on, sis,' Jodie said, throwing an arm over her taller sister's shoulders and giving them a squeeze. 'Let's blow this joint.'

Two hours later, Jodie stood with her nose up against the airport window. When she could no longer see Louise's plane winging its way back to London, she thought her legs might finally give way. A wave of warmth hit her from behind and she turned to find Heath, one hand resting an inch behind her back, just in case.

'Are you ready to go?' he asked, his voice kind.

She nodded and when he put his arm around her shoulder her head sank against him in relief. She was too emotionally drained to stop herself.

His dusty black Jeep was parked on the top level of the airport car park, an expanse of ugly grey concrete where heavy hot winds whipped about their faces. It was dry, characterless, the view nondescript, could have been a car park in any city in the world, and it represented the feeling in Jodie's heart perfectly.

'You'll see each other again,' Heath said, his deep voice rumbling through his chest and hers.

Jodie nodded, lifting her heavy head away from the comfort of his chest. 'I know. But it still hurts.'

He dropped his arm to reach into his pocket for his keys and Jodie felt strangely bereft. In self-protection she moved a good foot away from him, and even though it was a warm day she hugged her arms around herself to stave off a shiver.

Heath twirled the keys on the chain but didn't unlock the car. 'Are you really having second thoughts about staying here?'

Her emotions warred inside her, but her mind was made up. 'Lou was right. I would kick myself later on if I didn't give it my every effort to stay.'

'That's the best news I've had all day,' he said.

Jodie looked up to find him watching her with a warm, half bedazzled expression in his heavenly, sock-it-to-me, feel-them-all-the-way-to-your-toes blue eyes.

He leaned his lanky form against the car. 'So let's say we do this thing,' he said. 'You and me.'

She could have asked what thing, but she knew what he meant. She knew it with every fibre of her being. His lazy question shouldn't have been so completely overwhelming considering how they had met, and considering the way they had been flirting with the idea in every conversation they had had to date. But still Jodie felt her heart growing beautifully large in her tight chest.

Heath stuck the key in the door, and then took both of her hands in his. She could feel the pulse beating hard and strong in his thumbs. He was just as overwhelmed as she, but he didn't falter. He smiled down at her, his beautiful blue eyes thawing every last cool, aloof, closed-off place inside her until she was putty in his hands.

'Jodie Simpson,' he said, 'will you marry me?'

As all remaining breath drained completely from her, she gripped his hands tight and made the tough decision.

In the beginning she'd thought that a two-year deal would be an incentive to any number of guys. But without *those* guys banging on her door, she would have to settle for something different, for reasons more subtle.

Barnaby the visual merchandiser would give her away in a second. Scott would send her around the bend. If she wanted to do this, to find a guy whom the immigration authorities would actually believe that she had fallen madly in love with and married within a month of meeting, Heath was the one.

And all the other stuff, the fact that he lived beyond the black stump and she loved the urban jungle, the fact that she was after a two-year deal and he was after the real deal, yet after two years she *would* say goodbye, all that stuff would have to be dealt with as they went along.

'Yes,' she said, her voice coming out way stronger than she felt. 'I will.'

CHAPTER FIVE

JODIE stood before a celebrant at Melbourne Town Hall, repeating Heath *Connor* Jameson, over and over in her mind.

She wore no veil, and no typical wedding dress, just a butter-yellow strapless sundress that swished about her knees as she walked. Her hair was curled and pinned loosely at the base of her neck, and she wore a pair of tiny yellow daffodil-shaped studs—the first she had ever made.

Lisa and Mandy stood as witnesses as agreed, but she hadn't counted on Heath inviting his whole family: brothers, sisters, in-laws, toddlers, and even a couple of distant aunts had come along for the big show. All Jodie kept thinking was that if she and the man at her side had managed to mis-understand one another on the details of their wedding day, what else would she have to fight him on further down the line?

When they had agreed on a simple civil

ceremony in the city, she had pictured the two of them, Lisa and Mandy, and a few drinks with local friends at The Cave afterward. But all this family made the wedding feel real.

Jodie had never been one of those little girls who dreamt of her wedding day. At thirteen her father had left in the middle of the night. The next day her mother had screamed the house down at Jodie's crying, because it was unlikely 'that man' was her real father anyway. That night Patricia had gone into psychiatric care for the first time. And Jodie's life from that moment on had been 'real' enough.

A Jameson baby hiccuped somewhere behind her and she had to sniff in a great stream of air through her nose to stop from passing out.

'Breathe,' Lisa whispered beside her. She did as she was told and filled her tight lungs.

The celebrant cleared her throat and Jodie looked up to find her looking back at her expectantly. Lisa gave her a nudge and took the small bouquet of daffodils and mouthed the words, 'I do.'

Jodie felt the words come out of her own mouth, but only through the haze of surprise that she of all people had found herself in this position—a child of divorce, of uncertain paternity, of an imprudent mother whose genes ought never to be propagated further.

'And I don't think that it would be necessary for us to fulfil all of the usual marital obligations,' she had told Heath, while laying down the ground rules one night on the phone.

'You mean no sex?' he threw back at her, his voice all but crooning down the telephone wire. 'For anybody?' Jodie had to clamp a hand into the couch fabric to stop from swooning.

'Well, no. I'm sure there *will* be sex. Elsewhere. I just don't think it would do either of us any good to let our friendship move in that direction. It would only further complicate an already complicated situation.'

'Especially since you have already drafted up the divorce papers, right?'

'Right,' she said, happy he had arrived on the same page at last.

'But then again,' he said, and Jodie's teeth clenched again remembering the moment she had lost him, 'I'm sure that a year ago neither of us would have answered an ad for someone looking for a husband in a hurry. Circumstances change. Life throws down opportunities that we don't see coming. Never say never, right?'

'Well, then, at least let me pay you,' she said, moving onto a subject that she had thought might be the more uncomfortable of the two subjects but it now somehow seemed less delicate.

'For sex?' he said back. 'But I thought you just said—'

'No! Not for sex. As a kind of betrothal endowment.'

She still had some savings, and some money coming in from sales of her earrings to Mandy's voracious friends. And she could cash in her return ticket for a thousand dollars at least. Jodie couldn't officially work just yet, but she didn't want to be a burden on Heath. She wanted to help with the household expenses. She needed him to hang in there for two years. And to a poor farmer, a betrothal endowment made sense.

Though he had kind of talked her around in circles on that issue too until she couldn't remember what the final outcome had been.

But now, here she was standing at the altar next to a guy with sexy unkempt hair and flirtatious eyes, looking all too dashing in a dark suit, white shirt and yellow tie, who had all but admitted that he wasn't averse to the idea of sleeping with her. And, truth be told, she wasn't all that averse to the idea herself.

Will-power, she reminded herself. *Self-control*. It would be up to her to keep things congenial but not consummated.

Suddenly Heath took her by the hand, and she almost leapt out of her shoes in fright. He tugged her to face him and he winked, discreetly enough for only her to see, and she even managed a wobbly smile.

A cool white gold band appeared from nowhere on her ring finger and the glimmer and sparkle of the new jewellery took what little breath she had fair away.

When Heath had offered to look after the rings, she'd agreed, insisting only that he not give her some family heirloom. She had been expecting a simple yellow gold band, a quickie special, not white gold engraved with a delicate wreath of intertwined Lancaster roses and Australian wattles.

English roses…

A bitter taste rose in her throat as she wondered for the umpteenth time how she was going to tell her mother. It wasn't her fault that Patricia had gone away and not turned on the answering machine Jodie had bought for her before she had left. It wasn't her fault that, though Patricia sent sporadic postcards from whichever exotic locale she was in this week, she never gave a return address.

But then again, if her mother kept this up, maybe she would never have to tell her. Maybe over time Patricia wouldn't notice that she had overstayed her visa and would one day think, *Oh, well, glad she's happy where she is,* and that would be that.

Jodie bit her lip to stop herself from laughing hysterically at the thought of Patricia acting so calmly about anything. Divorce, marriage, the weather...

Then Heath, in his deep, familiar, soothing voice, promised to love and cherish her for ever and all thoughts of her mother were lost beneath a whole new set of worries.

As she numbly took her turn to slip a larger white gold band—this one plain and simple—on Heath's hand, she realised his ring finger had been broken and not set quite right at some time in the past. And she, the woman about to become his bride, had no idea how it had happened.

It took some doing to get the band over his large knuckle and in the end he had to help, much to the delight of those watching.

'You may kiss the bride,' the celebrant said, and Jodie heard *those* words loud and clear.

A kiss? Were they at that part already? Surely it was passé to have to kiss the groom at the end of a ceremony these days. But with twenty-one of Heath's closest family members looking on she could hardly voice a complaint. It seemed Heath had no intention of doing so either.

In a move that felt more real to her than anything else that day, Heath ran a reassuring hand through her curls. He then pulled her near, until she found herself bodily against him, chest to chest, hip to hip, and physically closer than the two of them had ever been.

She could see flecks of navy and silver in his bright blue eyes, she could see an old scar in his eyebrow, and she could see every gold-tipped chestnut eyelash.

'Just a quick warning—I am about to kiss you, Mrs Jameson,' he whispered with his mouth mere inches from hers.

'Get on with it, then, Mr Jameson,' she whispered back.

And then he kissed her. She expected a quick meeting of mouths, a platonic sealing of a bargain. But what she experienced was something else entirely.

The very moment their lips met Jodie was overcome by an explosion of sensation. Shivers and warmth all at once. Trembling fingers. Tingling feet. Hot limbs. Hot lips. Heat shooting through her centre.

Somewhere amidst all this searing awareness she felt him pull her closer still, or maybe she was the one who melted against him, until her entire weight was held by his strong arms like a heroine in an old movie.

When he released her, she let go with an audible sigh, and only then did she hear the outbreak of applause erupting around them. A wolf-whistle that could have only come from Mandy rocketed through the small room. Many of them were obviously under the impression that it was all real.

She swallowed over the lump in her throat, and if her insensible lips had been able to form the words she would have shouted them down then and there. 'This isn't real!' she would have said. 'We made a deal. Two years. Just two years.'

She looked up into Heath's eyes, expecting to see the same shock registered there, but her own shock was further compounded by the fact that she did not. His gaze was brimming with questions, but not surprise. It was as though he had expected the kiss to be exactly how it was, and he wanted more.

Before Jodie had the chance to remind him exactly why it would be for the best if he *didn't* get any more, she found herself stepping down the aisle with Heath's large hand in its unfailing position against her lower back.

When she stepped out into the early December sunshine she was hit with the most beautiful blinding array of rainbow-hued soap bubbles, as somebody had supplied each guest with a small clear tube of liquid soap. Then, before she had even had the chance to decide if she was delighted or cross, Heath led her to the roadside where an elegant horse and cart awaited them.

'What's this?' she asked, backing up.

'This, my lady, is our transportation.'

'But I didn't agree to this,' she hissed. 'To any of this. To the suit, or the guests, or the bubbles or…' *Or the kiss,* she thought. 'Or this,' she said instead, flapping a frantic arm at the docile Clydesdale horse.

'For Pete's sake, just get in,' he muttered. 'For one second pretend it's real and you just might enjoy it.'

She heard the frustration in his voice, and she didn't blame him. She was being overly touchy. So, to keep the peace, at least until they were out of listening range of their guests, she hopped into the handsome cab.

Heath leapt up next to Jodie, and motioned to the driver to get a move on. So much for the spring in his step when he had leapt out of his hotel bed that morning. To think he had even caught himself whistling when he was shaving, simply because it was his wedding day.

And now he was married he felt shell-shocked. Dazed. Confounded by the events that had changed and would further change his life. And it didn't help that his bride looked ready to either faint or spit chips at any given moment.

Well, blow her and her skittish ways, he

thought, determinedly wrapping an arm about her shoulders and drawing her to him.

He liked Jodie. Hell, he more than liked her. He was taken with her, a little enamoured, even, if he was honest with himself, which was obvious considering he was blithely ignoring her assertion that it would all be over within two years.

If she was in fact right, and at the end of two years they went their separate ways, then so be it. At least he would never look back on his life and say he had never tried. But if they didn't go their separate ways, if somehow the feelings that he had around her continued to grow at the rate they had, and if he was able to convince her that such feelings of her own were okay, well, then this day would be a decision well made.

If she wanted to fuss and fidget and complain, she could go right ahead, but he wasn't going to live those first two years walking on eggshells. Especially now, on this glorious summer day, trotting beneath the overhanging oaks on a Melbourne city street with the sun on his back and a beautiful woman at his side, he wasn't going to let anything take away his contentment.

'Have we made a big mistake?' Jodie asked, throwing a big bucket of cold water over his indomitably cheery mood. 'Have we gone into this for all the wrong reasons?'

He took a breath and counted to ten in his head. 'Jodie, we want the same thing. We both want to be married. And since we are agreed on that, and have said so in front of everyone, our motives beyond that point are irrelevant.'

'Irrelevant? You are from a large family, Heath. And you will want one of your own, if not now, then soon. I know it. But I have no interest in having a family. In being a part of a family. All family means to me is adversity or desertion. I want a Permanent Visa and nothing more. And I don't see either one of us budging on those issues.'

It took all of his strength not to throttle her then and there. He'd thought he knew how to deal with women. He had four sisters. The local police officer was a woman and they got on fine. He'd never had a problem with women at university— in fact he'd been somewhat of a big man on campus in that regard.

But Jodie was something else. She was wilful, determined and intractable. But she had such a consuming aura of vulnerability that those other traits shimmered just outside his mind's eye until they hit him like a slap across the face the moment he stopped paying attention.

Heath rubbed at his temple with the thumb and forefinger of his spare hand. 'We have time, Jodie.'

'Time?' she repeated, her voice becoming a little hysterical as she sat back and glared at him, her green eyes overbright. 'Are you saying that some time over the next two years you plan on convincing me to give in and live your great Australian dream? Well, no farm boy with dreamy blue eyes and the ability to wear jeans like no other man I've ever known will change my mind on all that.'

She came to an abrupt halt, her breathing shallow and loud, and Heath heard the moment she realised what she had said.

So she thought he looked good in jeans, did she? Well, well, well. It seemed Miss Prim-and-Proper English Rose was not as immune to him as she made out. And if her ardent response to his kiss hadn't given her away, the pretty pink blush warming her cheeks now did.

So he threw another log onto the fire to see how she would burn. 'Jodie, I meant there is time to call it quits.'

Her wide eyes were suddenly so full of concern he almost laughed in her face. Or kissed her. Either way she frustrated him to distraction.

'Are you saying you want to get our marriage annulled?' she asked, her voice more than a little breathless.

'No, Jodie, *I* don't. *I* happen to think this can work.'

Did he really? Seriously? Was he really willing to put all of his eggs in one basket with this flighty, skittish, crazy, adorable, intriguing, sexy woman now that she was giving him one final out? You bet he was. Marissa's death had taught him that if he wasn't willing to take risks he wasn't willing to live, and, boy, did this wife of his let him know he was alive.

'Stay, Jodie,' he said, putting every ounce of that resolve into his words. 'Stay and be my wife.'

She gave a great heaving sigh. And if he hadn't known any better he would have thought that, despite her constant protestations, this grand plan of hers was fuelled by more than a little romance.

'Okay,' she said, before he had the chance to push home any such advantage. 'I'm glad we have that settled.'

If they ever actually got to the end of the first day, this was going to be a heck of an interesting two years. The merry whistle started up again inside his head.

'Come here, you,' he said, and pulled her back in to snuggle at his side. She acquiesced, even going so far as to rest a gentle hand on his chest. He wondered if she could feel the immediate quickening of his heart.

A soft whisper escaped Jodie's lips and he looked down to find she had fallen asleep in his

arms. Her lashes rested against her pale pink
cheeks, her bow lips pouted as she breathed, her
tiny hand curled around a button on his white
shirt. And he knew in that instant he had made the
right decision.

There were farmers' daughters aplenty who
would have salivated at the thought of living at
Jamesons Run. But he had never been able to
convince himself to pick one of them and be
done with it.

Because for so very many years, since he had
returned from university and taken over the
running of the Run, he had wanted more. More
what, he had never been entirely sure. But definitely more.

And Jodie had *more* going for her in spades.

Two hours later, after being swamped by what
turned out to be not twenty-one but at least a
thousand and twenty-one Jamesons, most of
whom seemed to think she was the greatest thing
to happen to Heath in for ever, Jodie managed to
find herself at The Cave bar alone with an empty
martini glass and a drunk olive.

'Can I buy you a drink?' Heath asked, slipping
onto the stool next to hers.

'Why the heck not?' she said, the volume of her
voice proving that she was very slightly sloshed.

'I guess now is as good a time as any to find out what your favourite drink is.'

'Yours is beer,' she said, proudly. 'Whereas I don't think I actually have a favourite. But another of these would go down well,' she said, tipping her martini glass at him. 'You have one big family—do you know that?'

Heath looked over at the group huddled around a pair of pool tables. 'I don't see them nearly as much as I would like. They all live down this way now and have families of their own. Mostly at Christmas. Funerals…'

Funerals. The way the word seemed forced from deep inside of Heath made Jodie think of his brother's wife. Cameron, Marissa's husband, was the only one who hadn't come to the wedding. And even with the thousands of family members there, she could tell that Heath was more affected by Cameron's non-presence. She wondered if there was more to Cameron not being there than the recent loss of his wife.

But it was a fleeting thought. Jodie was feeling all warm, mushy, and vodka-logged, so she reached out and laid a hand over Heath's. 'So go hang with them. I'm fine sitting here, watching the world go by.'

Heath motioned to the bartender for the same for Jodie and his favourite beer for himself. Then he laid his spare hand over hers, turning it until it was palm up, cradled between his warm hands with his thumb running back and forth along her lifeline.

'That's all well and good,' he said, his voice travelling as a deep hum over the giggles and cackles of the restaurant crowd, 'but, still, I would prefer to sit here, with you, and share a drink.'

Jodie's breaths grew shallow, moving in and out with each stroke of his thumb. 'I don't think Elena much likes me,' she admitted before she knew the words were going to come out of her mouth.

'Rubbish,' Heath said, though he wasn't looking her in the eye as he said it, but glaring in the general direction of his older sister. 'Elena is the one who put me onto you in the first place.'

'Really?' she asked, seriously surprised at that nugget of information. Of all the happy Jamesons, Elena hadn't cracked a smile all day. But maybe Jodie had been wrong about her.

'Anything else I need to reassure you about?' Heath asked. 'I can't keep my eyes off you, you look so stunning. And you smell utterly delicious. I wish we were alone right now so I could—'

Jodie cut him off quick smart before her pink cheeks turned ruby-red. 'I'm good. Fine. Fabulous. A nap and a martini has become my new cure-all.'

'Really? Because I seem to remember you being a little shaky earlier.'

Jodie was all prepared to disagree, but Heath was looking at her with such concern she couldn't. Especially since that look reminded her very much of the one that had met her gaze as she had woken earlier from a heavenly slumber perched in the crook of his arm.

'Weren't you? Shaky?' she asked.

His mouth hooked into a crooked smile. 'Not a bit.'

She shifted on the stool until she was facing him fully, their knees knocked and she instinctively shuffled back as far as she could. 'But don't you think it's weird that I've never seen your home? I don't even know when you lost your first tooth or what you ate for breakfast. And here we are—Mr and Mrs.'

She threw her arms out as her voice grew ever so slightly hysterical. 'This is all about appearances,' she said, setting him straight as to the reason behind her fretting, or at least a reason she was prepared to admit. 'The appearance of a whirlwind romance between a London girl and an Australian farmer. At some stage, who knows when, we will get a visit from the Department of Immigration and the more we know about one another, the better.'

'Hmm. I look forward to getting to know all about you, too,' Heath said, a definite twinkle in his eyes as he rearranged his large form on the chair until Jodie was sure he had in fact inched closer to her. 'For the sake of the Department of Immigration.'

The bartender brought their drinks. Heath offered his for a toast and Jodie tapped the edge of her glass against his frosty bottle.

'So ask,' he repeated. 'Ladies first.'

There were so many questions tumbling around in her somewhat squiffy mind, so, in order to get warmed up, she picked an easy one. 'What *did* you eat for breakfast this morning?'

Heath laughed, throwing his head back and exposing his glorious tanned throat, with a perfectly sized Adam's apple that the funeral director would have killed for. His response was so liberated and so unexpected that Jodie found herself grinning back at him.

'Pastries,' he finally said. 'Three different kinds. Scrambled eggs. And a seasonal fruit platter. I had room service, remember. At home I don't get much more exciting than poached eggs, toast and coffee.'

'Right. But, okay, you answered, so now it's your turn.' She prepared herself for an equally endearing question and her smile muscles even began to twitch in anticipation.

But when he asked, 'Why me?' she was floored.

'Excuse me?' she said after taking three large gulps of her martini.

'I understand why you wanted to marry so quickly, but what I want to know is, of all the guys you met, and all the guys you have passed on the street and talked to and flirted with and endeared yourself to all the nights of your life before and after we met, why me?'

She blinked rapidly, trying desperately to find a reasonable reply to a question that she had never truly been able to answer herself.

'If you seriously plan on giving up on us after two years, why choose me?' he asked again. 'Am I that repellent that you see me as someone easy to ditch?'

Repellent? Hardly. But she needed to buy time. 'Do you want a cute answer or the truth?' she asked.

He leaned toward her, resting his chin on his palm, and Jodie felt his solid thigh slide alongside hers.

'The truth every time,' he said.

Then, as if the gods had organised it for her, Jodie spotted her neighbour Scott trying to chat up Lisa in the corner while Mandy and rotten Jake watched in delight.

'You seemed the least likely to flip out during a full moon and go on a killing spree,' she said in a mad rush of inspiration. 'And the least likely to be caught trying on my clothes.'

'And that's not the cute answer?' Heath asked, and she saw his confidence slipping just a little.

'It's both. Scott!' Jodie called out, waving madly.

Scott looked up, grinned, and then came scooting over, wiggling his thin hips in time with the music. Jodie could have kissed him when she saw he was decked out in a tiger-print Lycra top and black denim.

'Scott proposed to me before you did,' she said under her breath.

The closer Scott came, the higher Heath's eyebrows rose. 'So it was between me and him?'

'Mmm-hmm,' she said, biting her tongue to stop from laughing out loud. 'Scott,' she said when he neared. 'How are you?'

'Great! Thanks for inviting me, babes,' he said, going in for a lip lock.

Jodie turned her cheek at the last minute and managed to avoid a full-frontal attack. 'Scott,' she said through mushed lips, 'I would like you to meet my husband, Heath.'

Heath stood and gave Scott a manly handshake. 'Nice to meet you, Scott,' Heath said, his voice a good octave lower than normal.

'Ah,' Scott said, backing away and rubbing at his squashed right hand, 'the other man.'

'Scott,' Jodie said in warning. 'Be good.'

Scott held up his hands in defence. 'I am. I will. So she's protecting you already, is she?' he said, suddenly siding with Heath. 'Careful, she'll be a real mother hen if you let her. The number of times she has let me into the apartment building in the middle of the night when I forgot my keys while Mandy wouldn't have given a hoot—'

Jodie glared at Scott, doing her best to seem more like a fox ready to invade the chicken coop.

'Okay. Fine! I get it! Leave, Scott,' Scott said.

And Heath slowly slid back onto the stool as Scott scurried away.

'So does that answer your question?' Jodie asked.

'Several, in fact.'

Jodie's grin faltered as she found him glancing between her and Scott with a look of admiration in his eyes, and she wondered what more she had given away.

'Your turn,' Heath said, leaning across her to gather a handful of beer nuts. Jodie caught a waft of aftershave and the light remnants of shampoo and fresh cotton. She fought against taking a big deep breath. But it was too tempting.

Before she had the chance to discover if she had the guts to reciprocate his question, someone clinked a spoon against the side of a champagne glass and they were surrounded by a cacophony of tinkling glasses and people chanting, 'Kiss! Kiss! Kiss!'

Heath drew his eyes from the retreating back of Jodie's one-time suitor to the woman herself.

'Kiss! Kiss! Kiss,' the chant continued.

Well, if they insisted...

Being the good host he was, Heath reached out and took Jodie's hand, but was more than a little bothered when she stared up at him like a little lost lamb. Seriously! What was she so worried about? He was a nice guy. He had a fair idea that he wasn't all that hard on the eye. And he had been told more often than was probably polite that his kisses were pure sin.

If the kiss that had sealed their marriage vows hadn't sent all that home to the woman, then this kiss sure as heck would.

He hauled her into his arms, wrapping her surprised body tight. When her big green eyes looked up into his, full of apprehension and alarm, he growled so low so that only she could hear. 'Try to look like you're enjoying it, okay?'

She swallowed—her delicate throat moving in an enticing pulse. And when she nodded, he dived in.

Those lips of hers felt as good as he remembered. They fit perfectly against his, and they were oh, so soft and pliant. He was one lucky son of a gun to land himself a wife who was put on this earth for kissing.

She tasted even better than he remembered. The minty toothpaste flavour of earlier had made way for a mix of martini and appetizers. She tasted hot and spicy and as pure as fresh spring water all at once.

Wanting, needing, to get closer, he tilted his head and then, finally, finally, he felt her give in. Her delicate body melted against him, her small fingers softly curled into the hair at his neck, and with the sexiest soft sigh she was the one who then took the kiss to a whole new level of pleasure.

The kiss was suddenly not nearly enough. He wanted all of her. He wanted to undo the tempting zip that ran from her back to her hips. He wanted to watch as her dress pooled at her feet. And he wanted to touch, and feel, and kiss his way over every bit of delicious pale hidden skin.

But then it probably wasn't such a good idea as he had himself a cheering audience. Maybe this whole 'kiss her until her legs give out' thing wasn't such a rational move after all. He fought against the tumbling need to get carried away, while at the same time doing his best to repeat his weekly grocery list in his mind so that the kiss would remain G-rated.

When he pulled away, the echo of cheering returned him to consciousness. The kiss had only lasted ten seconds at the most yet it had felt as though he had been lost in her arms for an age.

Jodie's potent green eyes fluttered up at him as she came to—her pupils were large and dark and it took all of his strength not to throw her over his shoulder and carry her the two hundred kilometres back home.

When he disengaged his arms from around her, he felt her falter, so he caught her to him once again. 'Are you okay?' he murmured against her cheek, hiding his smile from her searching eyes.

'Not quite,' she admitted, and he was almost undone.

He helped Jodie back onto her stool and she was soon lost to him as a flurry of females surrounded her and ribbed her and she turned to a vision of blushing pink from within their huddle.

She glanced at him from within the mass of flailing arms and champagne glasses. Her brow furrowed for a brief moment before she smiled at him. And then someone stood in his way before he was able to return her enigmatic smile in full measure.

Heath touched at his lip with his forefinger, revelling in the taste of her still lingering there. It was absolutely certain that his wife was not nearly so unaffected by him as she would like. And in a day that had him feeling as confused as a bull with udders, that was a tiny but important ember of good news.

CHAPTER SIX

IT WAS after midnight by the time Jodie and Heath got back to the apartment.

Mandy and Lisa were staying on at The Cave. They said they were having too much fun to leave but Jodie knew better. Even Lisa had half fallen under Heath's spell and was hoping that they might have somewhat of a proper honeymoon night.

Such hopes only added to Jodie's exhaustion. It turned out that martinis on an empty stomach were not a good mix. Martinis were definitely *not* her favourite drink.

Okay, so lying had something to do with the hollow feeling as well. She had told so many lies that day that she couldn't keep them straight any more. Did she mean to honour and love Heath for ever as she had promised before everyone? Or was her two-year end goal still in place as strongly as it ever had been? Did she even have a clue?

The soft click of the front door told Jodie Heath

was inside, and they were all alone with the golden light of a couple of table lamps and the sound of Sinatra singing from the speakers. The kitsch romantic set-up was all Mandy.

Jodie flicked a switch on the wall, flooding the room with cold fluorescent light, before taking the cordless phone through her bedroom and into the joint bathroom. She shut both doors, threw her daffodil bouquet into the bath, took off her right earring, then sat in her usual spot on the bath's edge and called the one person who could be counted on to clear the ache in her head.

'Louise Valentine speaking,' her sister said down the line.

'Lou, it's Jodie.'

'Oh, Jodie, it's so nice to hear your voice. Thank you so much for the *Beach Street* DVDs. I mentioned I had them and a whole bunch of friends came around to watch on Saturday night. Did you know Angelo and Cait were actually twins? I didn't even see that coming.'

Jodie leant back against the cool wall tiles and let Louise's familiar accent soothe her. 'I'll keep them coming as long as they take your fancy.'

'Brilliant. You have no idea how they have kept me sane without you here to settle my nerves these last weeks.'

Jodie heard shuffling in the bedroom. It would

be Heath. He had kindly agreed to sleep on the couch for the time being, but he would still be keeping clothes and the like in her room.

'How's everything at home?' Jodie asked. 'Back to normal?'

'Normal? I'm not sure what that is any more. But everything is settling somewhat into a new sort of routine.' But Jodie heard that old weariness in Louise's voice that had dissipated with every day she had spent in Australia.

'Come on, Lou, you can tell me,' Jodie said, turning to face the gaudy floral shower curtain so as to distract herself from the zipping sounds in the bedroom.

'Well, Mum can still barely look at any of us she feels so guilty. And Dad still isn't well at all. Yet with the Bella Lucia empire expanding exponentially he isn't likely to find time to get better soon. I'm half afraid he's going to want me to help out in some way, and I'm more than half afraid that if he asks, I'll say yes. Though the last time I worked for the family it was a total disaster. Max and I fought continuously until he actually fired me. The brash bully.' Louise had to stop and draw breath. 'But none of that is half as interesting as my other news. I tried calling you last night to let you know, but you must have been busy. Prepare yourself...I have set up a meeting with our mother!'

Mother? The news hit Jodie like a lead shot to the stomach. Her fist closed so tight over her right earring, the thin clasp dug deep into the flesh of her palm.

'Patricia's back in London?' Jodie asked, so unexpectedly hurt that she hadn't heard so from the source.

'She is,' Louise said. 'She arrived back a few days ago, and the first thing she did was call me. I contemplated meeting her at one of the Bella Lucias but I think that might be a bit overwhelming.'

Kindest Lou, Jodie thought. Even though she was still not back on even ground with Ivy, she would not have flaunted Patricia in her face.

'We are meeting for afternoon tea on the top floor of the National Portrait Gallery. Some time next month, I'd say. It seems she is quite the traveller, and I'm sure I'll have a lot keeping me busy until then. Have you been? The view of Trafalgar Square is really quite breathtaking.'

'No,' Jodie gulped. 'I haven't. And how did Mum sound?'

'We only spoke briefly on the phone yesterday, but she seemed, in a word, charming,' Louise said.

Louise sounded so animated Jodie could not tell her how charming Patricia would be when it suited her. Patricia would charm a rattle from a baby when she had to, but the flip side to that talent was truly ghastly.

'I'm so glad, Lou,' Jodie said, trying to keep the mixture of emotions from her voice. *And Patricia has changed,* Jodie reminded herself. *With Derek in her life, and the right mix of meds keeping her stable, she has moved on, so now so can you.*

But her heart still ached nevertheless. Especially considering the next day she would be heading out to the land of snakes and spiders and flies and dust, hitching her skirt into her underpants to ward off desert heat, hanging out with the first real cows she would ever know apart from those she had seen on her dinner plate. Fate sure had a funny way of twisting things.

As though she could read Jodie's thoughts, Louise said, 'I wish you were here for this, Jodie, really I do.'

'Mmm-hmm.' Jodie reached up and ran a finger beneath her moist eyes. Right in that moment she wished she were there too, but she was in a mess of her own making.

'But that's not why you called,' Louise said. 'How's everything with you?'

Where to start? At the beginning. 'I got married today, Lou.'

Silence met her at the other end of the phone. 'Why didn't you tell me that was on the cards?'

Louise demanded. 'I would have been there in a flash.'

'Because you would have been here in a flash and you have enough going on back in the real world to worry about me. But now that it has actually come to pass, I didn't want to go a day without telling you.'

'Oh, Jodie, I am so happy for you. And so proud. You have gone and made your dream come true, and that is a rare thing indeed. So who is the lucky man?'

'It's Heath. The one who took you to the airport, remember?'

'Of course I remember Heath! Even in the state I was in, he was fairly unforgettable. Oh, good choice, Jodie, truly. Apart from being a total gentleman, he is absolutely dreamy. Heath is a man worth staying for.'

'Oh, no, don't you start. You sound like Mandy, who has conveniently forgotten that this never was a real romance. He's not why I am staying, Lou, and you know that.'

A distinctly male voice cleared his throat in the room next door and Jodie knew it was time to go.

'Either way, tell him all the best from me, will you?' Louise said.

'Shall do. Anyway, I'd better go.'

'Goodbye, sweetie. I miss you.'

'I miss you too.' Jodie fought to keep her tears from her voice. 'Bye, Lou.' And then Jodie slowly shut down the phone.

Then, before she had the chance to change her mind, she dialled in the international code and then her mother's home phone number. With every buzz of the dial tone she could feel the cold of the tiles seeping through the thin material of her dress and insinuating itself through every part of her body. But eventually the line rang out.

Damn it! Why didn't Patricia just switch on the answering machine? Her mother was impossible, that was why!

She wished the phone were old-fashioned so she could slam it down, but instead she had to get her kicks from pressing the off button with as much vehemence as she could focus in her index finger. The accompanying soft beep was hardly helpful.

She spun about, kneeled on the closed toilet seat to face the mirror and took a moment to clear the wobbly track of mascara running down her cheek and smooth down her eight-hour-old hairdo.

As she turned back she started when she found Heath standing in the now-open bathroom door. He still wore his black trousers and his white shirt was unbuttoned all the way through and hung loose at his hips. His feet were bare and his belt was gone. And she could do little but gawk.

What on earth was she doing with some hot blonde stud in her bedroom? How had *her* life come to this? And in such a way that she had demanded of herself a purely platonic relationship with said stud? What was wrong with her? How screwed up did a woman have to be?

'I knocked,' Heath said, his voice low in the quiet room. 'Twice. After I heard you hang up the first time. But you didn't answer. Is everything okay?'

Jodie nodded. But when she found herself fighting against a new wash of tears, she wondered if it really was.

Suddenly when everything she had wanted for so long had fallen into place, she felt as though it had spiralled out of her control. In marrying Heath she had gained herself an abundance of new family members who had welcomed her as one of their own, while the sister she really needed by her side was hurting and troubled back in the London she had so determinedly left behind.

Yet she had thought she was done with caring. She had cared so much for her troubled mother she had become certain there was not a drop of love left inside her to give to anyone else—except herself. She couldn't risk the fact that maybe she could care for another with such ferocity again, for surely that would sap her dry and she would disappear inside that love, an empty shell of a woman never to be found again.

It was all too much. As she sat on the toilet seat, in her beautiful yellow dress and her curls and the sunny scent of daffodils in her nose, her emotions ran over.

Her heavy head lolled against her chest and she buried her face in her hands as she began, in earnest, to cry.

Between her ridiculous unstoppable sobs she heard Heath swear under his breath and suddenly he was beside her. His knees cracked as he slid to the bathroom mat at her feet.

'Jodie. Sweetheart. What's wrong? What's happened? Who was on the phone? Is it your mum? Is she okay?'

She felt him reach out and lay a hand on her shoulder. It was gentle, it was kind, and it wasn't enough. She leaned into him until his arms enveloped her in a haven of warmth.

'It was Lou, on the phone,' Jodie said against his reassuring shoulder. 'She and Mum are meeting for afternoon tea.'

'And you won't be there to officiate,' Heath said, figuring out the guts of her concern in a heartbeat. If she was at her mulish best in that moment she would have huffed and puffed and given that shoulder of his a good whack. But she didn't have the energy.

'They won't need me to,' she conceded.

Heath slowly extricated himself from her clinging embrace until they were face to face. 'And that's a bad thing?'

He wasn't smiling at her as he usually did when she acted a little haywire; on the contrary, his face was a mask of serious concern, as though if he could soak up her pain in any way he would.

'No,' she said on a bone-tired sigh. 'It really is a wonderful thing. But it also makes me feel redundant.'

He reached up and tucked a stray curl behind her ear, his hand lingering at the back of her neck. 'Jodie, you are a big part of many people's lives, and not just those back in London.'

'I know,' she said, thinking of Mandy and Lisa and feeling weaker by the second as his fingers curled and twirled through the downy hair at the base of her skull.

'I don't know that you do. I don't know that you have a clue as to how important a person you already are in *my* life, Mrs Jameson?'

Mrs Jameson. The way Heath said those words Jodie had a brief glimpse into how important a woman could be in a man's life. Had her mum been that important in her dad's life before her moods and her unpredictability had driven him away? And if so, why was she now so determined to follow in her mum's footsteps?

The warmth of the small room, the bouquet wilting out of the corner of her eye, and the handsome groom kneeling at her feet created such ambience that her weak demeanour gave in to it all. All the confusion and mixed-up desires and the potent fact of Heath Jameson grew large in her mind until she couldn't stand it any longer.

She leaned in, bare inches, until her mouth gently met his. He tasted of salt. It took her a moment before she realised that was the taste of her own tears. Tears that made the joining of their lips slippery, and voluptuous, and as such the kiss quickly spiralled from comforting to something much more fervent.

Heath was so beautiful. So incredibly warm. And he wanted her. The tightness of his embrace left her in no doubt. A soft groan escaped her mouth as she slid from her seat to kneel on the bathmat in front of him, all the better to blend herself with him.

The warmth of his bare chest scorched through her thin dress and she pushed herself closer still, needing to brand her body and mind with such sensation to get her through the long lonely nights that would surely stretch ahead of her.

An age later, he pulled away to trail kisses over her face and neck.

'You're exquisite,' he whispered at the base of her ear and she all but blacked out with the pleasure of it.

She arched back to give him better access to whatever he wanted, to allow his enchanted lips to burn a hot trail over her desperately sensitive skin.

It felt so wonderful it almost hurt. Her throat had closed over with pleasure. She could barely breathe. In Heath's strong arms, with his kisses raining over her, she felt ravished, desired, worshipped, vital...

A great noise suddenly invaded her hazy senses as Mandy tumbled noisily into the apartment singing 'Going to the Chapel' at the tops of her lungs.

Jodie sprang apart from Heath like a teenager caught parking, but it was too late. Mandy and rotten Jake were standing gaping at the bathroom door.

'Oh.' Mandy giggled drunkenly behind her hand. 'Sorry. Didn't mean to interrupt.'

'Whoa,' Jake said. 'Jodes, babe, you look hot in yellow.'

Mandy slapped him across the chest, and all giggling ceased. She then grabbed him by the shirtfront, took her half-drunk bottle of champagne and began tiptoeing towards her bedroom.

'Pretend we're not here,' she whispered loudly. 'Go on doing whatever it was you were doing.'

When they disappeared into Mandy's bedroom with a bang of the door, the room was left again in quiet, the only sounds a faint whistle of wind at the windows, the hum of the fridge in the nearby kitchen, and their steady, louder-than-normal breathing.

Heath recovered first. Holding onto Jodie's hand, he got to his feet, then helped her up as well. She rubbed her knees, which, now that she was fully functional again, hurt from the hardness of the tiled floor.

'Are you okay?' he asked. His voice was husky and she could tell he was as shaken up as she was.

She nodded, though she wasn't sure *okay* described her current state. Her tears had dried up. Her headache was a mere memory. But she had been left with a yearning so deep she couldn't even hope to name it.

Tucking her hand behind his back, Heath drew her out into the lounge room in silence. It was a loaded silence. Jodie had no clue what to say. Whether to apologise for jumping on him, or remind him that she thought that indulging in such activities would only cause conflict later on, or simply give into the tingling sensation that had overtaken her from top to toe and say, 'What the heck? We're married; let's do it,' and blame an excess of martinis in the morning.

'I think it's time for bed,' Heath said and Jodie's knees all but gave way beneath her.

He moved past her to the safe side of the lounge chair, took the throw rug off the back of the couch, and shook it out and Jodie's heart lumbered back to a healthier pace. Only when he began to peel his unbuttoned shirt from his back revealing masses of lean, tanned muscle did Jodie move. But once she reached her bedroom door she turned, holding the frame for support, and said, 'Heath, thank you for today, and for the next two years, and…everything.'

It felt pathetically lacking considering the mix of emotions churning through her system, but Heath nodded graciously.

'You're welcome,' he said.

And on her wedding night, Jodie turned and walked into her bedroom—alone.

Heath walked around the apartment, turning off the table lamps and the stereo. And by the time he lay down, he felt as though he had run a marathon.

He grabbed the light blanket from the back of the couch and laid it over his prostrate form. It was a warm night; he wouldn't need any more coverings, but it would take more than a snug blanket to put him to sleep.

Blame it on the kiss. For what a kiss it had been. Jodie's hands had been all but ready to slide his shirt from his back and then some. He was certain he hadn't been imagining it, even if his desire for such an occurrence had been all but blinding him at the time.

But there was no way he was going to follow through on the promise of that kiss with Mandy and her beau on the other side of their bedroom door. Jodie was way too special for that. Such a union, in such a place, would only have been soured by morning.

A bump sounded in one of the bedrooms, followed by giggling and whispering. At least someone in the house would be getting some tonight. He laughed aloud, the cynical sound disappearing in the lofty room.

Most guys didn't really think much about their wedding day, about what they would wear, about who would come, about the band, or the flowers, as women tended to. But the wedding night, now that was something they held in high regard. And here he was, lying on a lumpy couch, his feet sticking over the end, dressed still in his wedding-day trousers so as not to frighten the several other inhabitants of his wedding-night accommodations, while his bride slept in the other room.

'Well, buddy,' he said out loud, staring at the flickering shadows on the wall, 'she never promised you anything more. So you have no one to blame for this but yourself.'

He rolled onto his side to block one ear against a cushion. Light from street lamps outside spilled through the big front windows. He could sleep through a full moon. But the bright golden hue of the fluorescent lights just didn't feel natural to this country boy, even against the backs of his closed eyelids.

Thankfully, the next night they would be at Jamesons Run for their 'honeymoon'. No matter how forgiving someone might be to the fact that when in town they lived with two other women, Heath had managed to convince Jodie that if they didn't at least spend some time by themselves after the wedding the whole thing would be labelled a farce by not only his family, but by any officials asking questions later on.

But the knowledge that tonight of all nights his lovely wife, the woman whose kisses sent him up in flames, was snuggled up in her bedroom mere feet away would be enough to keep his thoughts occupied and his eyes wide open for hours to come.

CHAPTER SEVEN

LATE the next morning, Jodie leant her head against the window letting the hum of the car thrum through her as they swept past scenes the likes of which she had never seen.

Gangly newborn sheep dotted numerous herds as they headed further into rural country, and she knew just how they felt. For the first time since she had left home and travelled the miles of land, air and sea to reach Australia, she felt displaced. She wasn't on holiday any more. But she didn't feel quite at home either.

Her life was changed. She was changed. And she saw the world around her through changed eyes. Dorothy wasn't in Kansas any more.

Cerulean-blue sky stretched as far as the eye could see. Sporadic puffs of perfect white clouds all but blinded her with their brilliance, as did grass the colour of wheat, dirt the colour of red wine, lonely grey gums and bottle-green willows dipping their branches towards large brown dams.

While back in London the days would be growing overcast, rainy and dark, in Melbourne it was only getting hotter and the days longer. And Christmas was coming.

Christmas had always been the best time of year in her London life. Somehow every year Patricia ended up with a windfall just before her Christmas Eve birthday. In celebration the two of them would take the half-hour public-transport trek out to the Kings Road in fabulous Chelsea.

They would walk the length of the famous old strip, window shopping, maybe even picking up a fancy new outfit or two, and stopping for tea at one or other of the old cafés, even passing by the Bella Lucia flagship restaurant without having an inkling of the family link behind that grand façade.

They would walk off their meal with a wander around the gardens at the back of the Royal Hospital where the Chelsea Flower Show was held each May. To Jodie that was the most beautiful place in the whole world, a secret garden with park benches engraved in honour of lovers young and old, flowers as far as the eye could see, the River Thames slinking by, and her mother contented and smiling.

Jodie never knew where the money came from each year. She had always kind of hoped it was from her father, but since Louise had shown up on the scene Jodie had had all sorts of horrible ideas that perhaps the Valentines had been paying hush money all along. From what she had gleaned from Louise they would be capable of such a deed. Either way she had never questioned it as it gave her one day a year of a real mother-daughter relationship.

Heath's black Jeep, his 'city car' as he called it, turned off the main road at a gap in a long horse fence, bounced over a cattle-grid, and then bumped along an uneven dirt track toward a wall of massive pine trees in the near distance.

'We're here,' Heath said, his voice low and quiet in case she had been sleeping.

She rolled her head back upright and sent him a guarded smile. He smiled back before turning his face to the front. His right arm rested along the edge of the open window, his soft hair flickered in the breeze, an easy smile rested on his lips. With the horizon as a background to his profile, lit by a different sun, breathing different air he looked like a different man. It was how one looked when one felt at home.

She turned back to face the front as they whisked through the tall green trees and on the other side of the enclosure stood a grand white two-storey wooden house with a silver roof and a wrap-around veranda. Past the house were a number of paddocks and to the right stables.

And beyond? Land as far as the eye could see. Wide flat red dirt scattered with random eucalypts leading away to a perfect hill in the distance.

Her 'home' had been a dingy little flat. She had slept on the lounge floor and then, when her father had left, her mother's only concession to the grief she had felt had been the gift of a second-hand single mattress. With a mother on sickness benefits there had been little more they could afford. But Jamesons Run, Heath's home, was magnificent.

'Oh, my, Heath,' she said, feeling a little breathless. 'This is just so beautiful.'

'You like it?' he asked, his voice unusually hesitant.

'How could I not? It's breathtaking.'

'It's miles from anywhere, and anything,' he warned.

And she knew he was thinking of her. Her city-girl tastes. But she'd never been one of these girls with a need to shop every day—she'd never had the money to do so anyway. The Christmas shopping sprees on the Kings Road in Chelsea had been to her like wishing on the first star—a way to remind herself there was hope beyond her four walls.

'So long as there is food, water, a table on which I can make my jewellery, and a phone with which I can call my friends, then I think I can cope,' she said.

He pulled the Jeep to an easy stop at the top of a circular dirt drive. Jodie opened the door and got out, stretching her tight, cramped limbs before a great yawn eased from her mouth, opening her lungs to the warm country air.

As she followed Heath and their luggage up the front steps she felt even more nervous than she had been before their blind date—nerves jangling and tongue-tied, all gangly limbs and expectation.

But this was worth all the nervousness—the thought of sleeping in Heath's family home, the forthcoming intensive bovine research in case she ever had to answer any questions about such parts of Heath's life, being away from Melbourne's delights for a few nights every week. The end result made it so.

Heath opened the front door and stepped back. As Jodie walked over the threshold, she had a vision of Heath scooping her up in his arms and carrying her through. And by the glimmer in his blue eyes and the crease in his right cheek she wondered if he was thinking the same.

It only made her hustle faster and she was over that threshold and into the foyer before either of them had the chance to blink.

But there her feet stopped.

If she'd thought the exterior of the Run was beyond her wildest dreams, the interior was a step further again. Before her was an honest-to-goodness waste-of-space foyer with nothing for ten feet either way bar a six-foot-long solid-oak hall table resting against a brick-red feature wall and holding a vase filled with three-foot-high dried Australian wildflowers.

Her feet slid slowly along polished wood floorboards as she eased herself around the stand-alone wall. As usual, she felt rather than heard Heath follow. She could always tell when he was near. His warmth? His woodsy scent? His comforting aura? Whatever it was, she skipped ahead into the sunken formal lounge so as to rid herself of the cloak of awareness wrapped about her.

As she moved about the room complete with red leather sofas, rugs that looked as though they cost more than she had ever earned in a year, and a massive wood fireplace, it hit her like a sack of flour to the head—Heath had money. Lots of it.

She hadn't even thought to ask. Didn't farmers struggle with things like crop failure and drought and government subsidies? Well, not this one. This one had flourished enough to support an extended family and a penchant for expensive furniture. It seemed the bookish young girl from the backwaters of London had married herself an outback land baron.

So much for her promise to pay him for services rendered. Heck, the thousand-odd dollars she would have got back from cashing in her plane ticket would be a drop in the ocean to a guy in his position. No wonder he had never again brought up her offer of a monetary inducement, as it had nothing to do with his continued determination to be married to her.

But why, if he was so prosperous, hadn't he asked for a pre-nup? It had never even occurred to Jodie. She owned a suitcase full of clothes, and a car so rusty it ought not to be on the road. So why? Had she been ignoring the truth all along—did he actually think that in two years' time she might actually change her mind?

She forced herself to keep exploring rather than to stand staring at each new opulent convenience, and wondering what other hidden delights, and secret motives, the man she had married had hidden up his sleeve.

Heath stood back and watched as Jodie moved through his home, her wide eyes taking in every little detail.

She liked it. She said it was beautiful. And those words had warmed him like a bonfire on a cool autumn night.

He hadn't realised how important her impression of the Run might be. In recent times, he had found the place too far from the world. Constrictive. Unvaried. The walls of his big old house made him antsy. The recent time spent in the city had felt like a relief. A way out. And Jodie had been a big part of that.

He let her be, heading off to the large master suite. He dumped their bags by the twin couches in the parents' retreat and tried to ignore the thirty-odd messages blinking back at him from the answering machine on the bedside table.

He'd been away only a couple of days. He'd seen most of his family during that time. What more could they possibly need from him? In an instant he felt the walls cramping in on him again. Whatever they wanted he would get to it later. Right now he had plenty else on his mind.

Staring at his big new king-sized bed, her 'we really ought not to consummate' suggestion came slamming back to him.

Okay, so he was frustrated on more than one level. He was a man after all. With needs. And desires. And overnight those desires had reached a point the likes of which he had never known. And for the one woman who had very decidedly told him that it would be better for him if it never happened.

He rolled his tense shoulders, shaking off the sexual tension that was binding his muscles in knots now that for the first time in such a long time they were alone without the threat of one or another of her housemates walking in on them.

His hands dived into his jeans pockets as he sauntered out of the bedroom, past the staircase, and through the lounge to the kitchen where the reason behind his great frustration stood running a hand over the granite bench.

'Finding your way around?' he asked and was surprised when she turned on him with an accusatory glance.

'You have a dishwasher!' she said.

Heath laughed, feeling his tension slipping in the face of her bewilderment. 'I do. Is there a problem?'

She blinked and shook her head. 'No, it's actually wonderful. I just didn't expect…this.' She swept an arm around his large kitchen gleaming with all the mod cons.

Why she didn't expect a single guy to go all out and have every electronic convenience at his disposal he had no idea. If he had to wash the dishes by hand every night, he very much doubted whether he would bother pouring his pre-made dinners onto a plate before eating them.

As though she had forgotten he was even there,

she continued through the swinging doors into the family room at the rear of the house. Her jaw dropped when she took in a pool table, discreet surround sound speakers, and wall-mounted LCD TV. She looked over her shoulder and seemed almost angry.

'Does this thing have a sports channel?' she asked, irately pushing random buttons on the remote.

'Several,' he said, leaning over to punch in the channel for ESPN.

She stared at the TV, her eyes flicking over the timetable of events darting across the bottom of the screen. 'Jeez,' she said in a long, slow drawl.

'What's the matter now?' he asked, his throat tickling with laughter. She really was the most unpredictable girl he had ever known.

'But where's the sawdust on the floor, and your grandmother's chintz lounge, and the matted old dog curled up on the lambskin rug by the hearth?'

'What on earth are you talking about?'

'I feel like I have walked into a pad in Soho, not a home in the middle of the outback.'

Heath finally caught up. 'Don't tell me you were really expecting kangaroos on the doorstep.'

Her soft pink mouth twisted as she thought about how to answer. 'Well, yes, actually.'

'Just as I would expect you London gals to

have regular lunches with the Queen and have haircuts straight from the eighties like the women who work for British Airways. Why is that?' he asked, taking the opportunity to move closer to her as he spoke. 'What is with the bad haircuts, and old-fashioned uniforms? Is it some sort of secret weapon so that when we unsuspecting international males finally meet one of you real London gals, we are blindsided by your perfectly contemporary beauty?'

Jodie blinked back at him, all gorgeous confusion, and mistrust, with just the tiniest hint of laughter beneath it all. And Heath knew that no amount of shoulder-rolling or keeping his hands tucked safely away in his pockets could force down the desire to touch her, hold her, know her as a husband ought to know his wife.

And at that moment the doorbell rang, sending chimes of his sister Jackie's favoured Mozart through the house. Heath's itchy fingers curled into tight palms. He wished he could continue this promising line of conversation with Jodie.

But the doorbell chimed again, and for someone to be at *his* door, to have come all the way up his drive, it would be important.

'Excuse me,' he said, his voice coming out unnaturally deep. He turned, clearing his pesky throat, before he answered the door to find Carol and Rachel Crabbe, cling-wrap-covered crockery dishes in hand.

Excellent. Mandy and Lisa were bad enough, but the Crabbe sisters? He had every idea that their intentions on intruding at exactly this time were nowhere near as innocent. But they were neighbours, and in a tight community such as this he had to be polite.

'Carol. Rachel. What can I do for you on this fine sunny day?'

'We've come to welcome your wife to the community,' Carol said.

Rachel tried peering around his shoulder. 'Is she in?'

Looking at them now in their matching floral dresses and low buns, he wondered how it had ever entered his mind that when the time came to find a wife one or the other of these women might do the trick.

'She is. We actually only just drove in from the city a few minutes ago. So now is perhaps not the best time—'

'Nonsense,' Carol said, using her broad shoulder to muscle Heath out of the way while the much smaller Rachel snuck through the gap at his back.

On a resigned sigh, he closed the front door and followed them into the lounge to find Jodie in the kitchen doorway with an apple halfway to her mouth looking from Rachel, who had taken up residence on one of his couches, to Carol, who busied herself putting the casseroles in the fridge as though she had done so a hundred times before.

Carol moved back into the lounge and pushed Jodie along in her wake with a firm hand at Jodie's back. 'Come sit,' she insisted.

Heath wandered more slowly in and watched and waited for the train wreck that would undoubtedly come.

'So,' Rachel said, her smile sickly sweet. 'How did you two lovebirds meet?'

'It was a blind date,' Heath said, joining Jodie on the couch. 'Elena set us up.'

'Oh,' Carol said, her face pinched as if she had swallowed a lemon. 'I am surprised Elena would have needed to look beyond the local township for such an endeavour.'

'Well, look she did,' Heath said, 'and she found me a winner.' He reached out, took Jodie's hand, and held on tight. He could feel the tension streaming from her. She knew that these two 'friendly neighbours' were only here so they could spread the word to the rest of the neighbourhood about Heath's new bride.

'So, Jodie,' Carol said. 'I assume you haven't had a chance to meet the horses as yet. Heath is a great lover of riding.'

Jodie shook her head. 'I've only met the furniture so far,' she said, and Heath choked back a laugh. Oh, Jodie knew exactly what she was dealing with.

'So which horse will be hers, do you think?' Rachel asked, batting her lashes and puckering her lips in his direction.

'I don't ride,' Jodie butted in.

The younger of the sisters raised a bushy eyebrow. 'You *don't* ride?'

'Sorry,' Jodie said. 'No. I really ought to have taken time out from croquet lessons and etiquette class.'

Heath watched her in mute fascination as her voice came out loud and imperious, perfectly resonant of the Queen's English and quite unlike her own, much more jaunty accent.

'But Mummy never deemed riding a necessary pursuit for a young lady in the quest for a husband nowadays.' She reached back and hooked her hand through Heath's arm and he had little chance but to go along with her odd charade. 'And as it turned out, she was right.'

'So that's the trick,' Rachel said, smiling sadly at Heath, who wasn't quite sure how to react so kept his features schooled into the blankest expression he could muster while dying to laugh. Rachel was thankfully silenced when her older sister shot her the evil eye.

After five minutes more of off-the-wall pleas-
antries, the Crabbe sisters showed themselves out.
Heath had never managed to have them stay for
less than two hours, and he was utterly thrilled
that the addition of Jodie to his home seemed to
have put a nix on that little inconvenience for
ever.

Or the time being at least, he thought, feeling
crabby all of a sudden. For ever certainly had a
nicer ring to it.

Once the sisters' car was so far in the distance
he could no longer see their dust, Jodie begged,
'Please tell me that is not your version of the
welcome wagon?'

'No. That is our version of the ugly stepsisters.
Though I have the feeling they won't come
around without an invitation next time.'

'I know I ought to have held my tongue as they
are your neighbours, but they were hardly
backward about being forward themselves.'

'They're your neighbours now too.'

With a groan, Jodie buried her face in her
palms. 'The whole township will know by now
that your new wife is nothing but a stuck-up boor
who can't ride a horse.'

'So what?' he asked. 'I thought you wouldn't
care what others think.'

'Yeah? Well, it turns out I do care,' she bit back,

now looking him dead in the eye. Slight chin squared, her bright eyes flashing with indignation.

He fought the urge to lean over and kiss the expression from her adorable face. But in such a mood she was as likely to slap him as not. So instead he moved out of range, heading down the front steps, hoping she would give into curiosity and follow.

Jodie watched Heath amble away from the house for five seconds at most before jogging after him. 'How about you introduce me to your horses so the next time I am asked I don't make such an ass of myself?'

She was mighty happy to change the subject. It had been jealousy, pure and simple, that had led her to puff out her feathers. If she had come from nowhere to marry the man that doe-eyed Rachel Crabbe had wanted for herself, then she was the one who ought to have left feeling guilty, not Rachel. And by Heath's reaction she was fairly certain he would have pinned her motives in a heartbeat. But either he was too much of a gentleman, or hopelessly oblivious.

When they reached the stables one of the horses ambled over to say hello. She reached out and ran a tentative finger down the nose of the massive bay. 'So who's this?'

'Esmeralda.'

Jodie blinked, then looked over the stable door and checked between the large horse's legs. 'But it's a boy horse,' she whispered.

Heath laughed. 'You don't need to whisper. He knows he's a boy. And to answer your next question, after my parents died, I promised my littlest sister Kate that she could name the next foal that came along. She was fourteen and I thought she needed something positive to focus on. Then out came this brute, and Esmeralda he was.'

'From *The Hunchback of Notre Dame*?'

'Mmm. I have often dreamed that she had been so taken with *Aladdin* instead.'

Heath held out a hunk of broken carrot on the flat of his hand and Esmeralda nipped it into his big soft mouth in one bite. Heath held out another chunk to Jodie, who shook her head. She was happy to watch.

'What was it like growing up in a large family?'

Heath raised an eyebrow. 'Great. Never having your own room. Fighting for seconds at dinner. Girls hogging the bathroom. For evermore having people depend on you for every little thing. A big family is *precious*.'

Jodie knew he was kidding. The fact that so many of them had come to the wedding proved that. His family was everything to him.

'How about you?' he asked, slipping through

the swing door to give Esmeralda a pat on his massive flanks. 'What was it like with just you and your mum?'

'Similar in a way. When family calls, I can't say no either,' Jodie said, not wanting to admit to him how hard it had been. But he was watching her with that wide open face of his. *The truth every time,* he had once told her.

'It was tough,' she said, finding the admission less forced than she would have imagined. 'She needed constant care, and someone else to give her boundaries, as she was completely unable to enforce them on herself. But Mum has held up really well since I've been away and for that I will be for ever grateful to her new husband Derek.'

I only hope he can keep it up. I only hope she doesn't exhaust him with her neediness and changeability. I only hope he loves her enough to overlook those things because if he ever falters, if she ever sees a chink in his armour...

No. Her mother would just have to be grown up enough to make it work. She just had to!

'And do you think Louise will stay in London now?' Heath asked.

'Yeah. She will. She has a lot of ties keeping her there. Her other family is there, and her work. And she has a lot of sorting out to do on both counts, which she can't possibly do from here.'

'Well, it sounds as though things are working out well for everyone. So let's hope none of them call you home then, hmm?'

Though he was busy brushing down Esmeralda's nose, Jodie heard the edge to his voice. He was saying he wanted her to stay. Not just because he was a nice guy and he knew she was wishing and hoping for it to be so. But for his own reasons. Of that she was becoming more and more sure. Perhaps he wasn't nearly as oblivious as she had hoped.

The kiss the night before had been an aberration. An exquisite aberration borne of emotional highs and lows that she would always treasure. Now if they only kept their friendship intimate enough to make their marriage appear real, but aloof enough to keep their emotions intact, they would be fine. If only...

Jodie watched as Heath led Esmeralda to a yard nearby, and, looking as she was at his left hand, she noticed he was not wearing his wedding ring. She blinked. But the image remained the same. Her world tilted at an odd axis for several seconds before crashing back into place.

Okay, she said to herself, *relax. You are at home—his home—in the middle of nowhere with no one to notice such things bar you and the cows. So what's the big deal? It's not as though some immigration officer is going to jump out from behind a water tank and see it.*

So why did the sight make *her* feel so very, very let down?

Because, damn it, the upset she felt at him not wearing his wedding ring had nothing to do with some strange immigration officer and nothing to do with the appearance of being happily married to the Crabbe sisters and their like. And it had everything to do with his desire to be married to her.

Somewhere in the back of her mind, since this whole thing had begun, Jodie had had the feeling that Heath was not just in this marriage to do her a favour, or to keep the local girls and his busybody sister at bay, but because maybe, just maybe, this big, beautiful, kind man actually had feelings for her.

And even though it was the very last thing she had wanted to find in her temporary husband, she had been hooked. Addicted. Enamoured of the feeling that it might be true. The romantic little girl who wished on stars, and found simple pleasure scampering unimpeded through daffodils, had been whispering sweet nothings in Jodie's ear until she had given in and married the one man of all those she had ever met for whom she had feelings as well.

So much for being emotionally aloof. Stupid, stupid Jodie.

'I'm actually feeling a little off all of a sudden,' she said, backing away. 'Why don't you take him for a good long ride, and I'll make myself a cup of tea and watch the Chelsea match which is about to start on that ridiculously big TV of yours?'

But before he even had the chance to say if it was all right with him, she turned and stormed back to the house before she said anything more incriminating.

CHAPTER EIGHT

THERE was no way Heath was going to chase Jodie inside while his hands were full with a restless stallion. So he took her words at face value, grabbed his Akubra hat, leapt up into the saddle, tapped his heels into Essie's side and galloped out into the wide-open planes of the Run.

A good while later he slowed to a walk as his thoughts were anywhere but on the feel of the horse beneath him. They were tending back to the homestead, to the fact that he would have a woman waiting for him there. Though she was hardly waiting for him—more than a dozen burly soccer players would be keeping her occupied.

He didn't blame Jodie for running from him so suddenly to watch a game of football. If he'd had the choice of being right where he was, or being at a match in London, the big smoke would have won in a heartbeat. Well, okay, maybe not that easily. Atop his favourite steed, the midday sun consuming all shadows, and the muted red earth stretching as far as the eye could see, this moment was pretty spectacular.

But all he had ever wished for was the choice. With four siblings still in their teens, and three of those still in school, on the day his parents had died, there had been no alternative. He'd had to give up his life, so that they could have theirs.

If he had stayed in the city on the design end of stadiums, high-rise buildings, new parks and the current redevelopment of the city's docklands, and left his family to their own devices, would every one of them have earned a university degree? Without his backing would every one of them now own their own home? Would he and Marissa have stayed together, and as such would he and Cameron have remained close? Would they be on better terms now? Would Marissa be alive today?

No. He and Marissa had been friendly, but their relationship had been on the decline even before his parents' deaths. They had both used the distance as an excuse, but even if he had stayed on in the city they would never have lasted. And, worse, Cameron would have missed out on the past five years with the woman he loved.

The world had turned the way it had for a reason. He had stayed on at the Run, turning it from a comfortable homestead into a grand success, and his whole family had benefited. If Marissa's sudden passing had taught him anything, it was that his choices were his alone, and there was nothing to be gained by waiting for his life to happen.

The world turned, but if you didn't reach out and grab your opportunities by the scruff of the neck they would pass you by. Living on instinct and treating time like something to be grabbed, not something to be endured, he had met and married Jodie.

So why, rather than feeling as if his life was finally under his own control, did he feel as if his stomach were tied in knots?

Jodie hadn't left him with Esmeralda so she could watch a game of soccer. Something else had spooked her. Something else always spooked her. The pragmatic half of him wanted to keep riding until he had no choice but to sleep out under the stars. But the noble half of him wanted to turn back, to go to her, to be with her.

He had always thought himself excessively good at reading people. Heck, he could read her friends like an open book. Mandy, the loud one, was using noise to cover low self-esteem. Her relationship with that creepy Jake guy only cemented it. And Lisa, the gentle one, had taken so long to warm to him, and to warm to Jodie's impending marriage, he was certain she was nursing a broken heart and as such she saw the world as though through cracked lenses.

But Jodie? Every second of every day, he had a thoroughly new opinion of her. She could put his teeth on edge, then make his heart race within two blinks of those gorgeous green eyes of hers.

Oh, yeah, it had been weeks now since he had decided on a favourite colour. That exact shade of mottled jade-green that sparkled and glowered back at him by halves was for evermore imprinted on his mind. Green wavering between light and shade. Everything about Jodie bespoke of light and shade. She was luminous, yet had deep dark secrets, and that was what had drawn him to her in the first place.

Eventually, as he'd known deep down he would, he gave in to need and turned Esmeralda back towards home.

Later that afternoon, Jodie sat out on the veranda, her usual one leg hooked up beneath her as she sank into a mound of cotton-drill scatter cushions. The motion of the love seat took her slowly backward and forward as she hunched over a pair of jewellery pliers, a piece of fake mistletoe and a battery-operated flashing red bauble.

Weeks before, after a rather forgettable night of cocktails at The Cave, Mandy had persuaded Louise to get a belly ring as a way to stick it to her stuffed-shirt parents. And when the girls had found out that at age thirty-five it was Louise's first real act of rebellion, *ever*, it had become a bit of a running joke. So Jodie was making Louise a flashing mistletoe belly ring for Christmas.

When the last twist of wire slipped into place, she pressed the tiny hidden button in the side and the red bauble began to flash. It made her smile. But if it ever saw the inside of Louise's navel she would be much surprised.

She sighed lavishly as she looked out over the golden plains, surprised to see that the sun was that much lower than when she had begun. As it always had, working on the precise detail of her finicky work took her away from real life, made her forget every niggling worry that clogged her brain, and helped make the details of her life all the clearer.

And it was clear to her on that hot December day how far away from London she really was. The black cabs and double-decker buses, the tube, Piccadilly Circus and her beloved Chelsea football team all seemed as if they were in another world. Everything down here moved at a slower pace. Work, traffic, relationships. There was no rush. Everything happened in its own good time.

And all she had was time. Two years stretching out like the wide red land in front of her—vast, daunting, and unknown.

Through the red haze she saw a figure on horseback materialising out of the shimmering mirage above the hot, hard, crackled ground. Heath.

Somehow, in the last month, deep, warm, forever type feelings for Heath had snuck up on her so slowly she hadn't even seen them coming. That was why she had become so upset about the fact that he wasn't even wearing his wedding ring. Not because he didn't have feelings for her, but because she *did* have feelings for him.

As Heath came closer she could hear the thud of his horse's hooves on the hard, dusty ground. She was able to make out his lean form moving loosely and expertly with the cantering movement of the horse. His jeans were now brown with dirt. His worn Akubra hat was pulled low so that she couldn't make out his eyes. But she didn't need to see them to know their exact hue.

Jodie felt a sudden urge to leap out of the swing chair and head into the kitchen and what? Make tea? Tidy up? Hide? But there was nowhere to hide. Not physically. But emotionally?

Several minutes later, the porch door creaked, but Jodie knew Heath was near even before she heard him. The cloud of warmth he carried with him everywhere had enveloped her already. And her whole body lit up like a hurricane lamp to his mere presence.

She turned and her hopeless heart slammed against her ribs as she took in the view of jeans, white T-shirt, olive-green V-neck sweater pushed up to the elbows. And Heath. Freshly showered. Still-damp hair showing irregular tracks of his fingers.

His eyes were dark and fathomless in the afternoon light. He looked dangerous. But she knew he was only dangerous to her heart. He moved towards her. She thought again of leaping from the chair and running, but her foot hooked beneath her had fallen asleep.

He placed a cup of tea on the wicker table at her side, then tucked his hand deep into his trouser pocket, the other hand holding a cup of coffee for himself. 'Do you mind if I join you?'

'It's your house.' She knew she was being testy, but she had to keep a distance between them.

'What's mine is yours, Jodie. I promised you that in our vows and I meant it.'

'Right,' she shot back. 'But you never said that what was yours was so ridiculously much! I would feel more comfortable signing a post-nup if you know somebody willing to write one—'

He held out a hand stop her. 'Not interested.'

He was too trusting. People weren't all as nice

as he and his lovely family seemed to be. And she didn't want to be the one to teach him that lesson. People took advantage. People looked out for their own interests first. It was human nature. And he needed to be protected from that. He needed to be protected from her.

'Well, you should be. Really. Don't think you would hurt my feelings.'

'Jodie. Shut up,' he said, and only then did she hear the frustration in his voice. 'It's not going to happen.'

Of course. He was only following her lead. Her rotten disposition was as obvious as the blinking red light on Louise's belly ring. She only hoped that her temper had blinded him to all other undercurrents she had unearthed that day.

'What would an immigration officer say if they found out about such a document?' he asked, his blue eyes intense.

Well, that shut her up more than his demand had done. He was right. But she had the feeling that had been a convenient excuse not to engage in such an agreement.

He really, truly did not want to have a pre-nup. The guy was something else—a real, live, honest-to-goodness gentleman. Jodie had thought that her mum must have sold her soul to find the last one of those left on the planet.

Yet somehow she had managed to marry one too. What were the odds that the one man whom she had gone to great lengths to convince to be her husband in name only would turn out to be the most authentic man she would ever be likely to meet?

'Oh, just sit, will you?' she demanded, fluffing a hand at the deep wicker chair in the corner of the porch.

He sat, but in the swinging seat beside her. She moved her tingling foot down to swing beneath her as the chair rocked under his heavier weight.

'Did you finish your exploration?' he asked, resting a casual arm along the back of the long seat.

Jodie leaned forward to get her cup of tea, but more to avoid any unnecessary brush of his arm. 'I did, thanks.'

After the second half of the Chelsea game, which they'd lost, Jodie had spent a downhearted couple of hours checking out the rest of the house, taking notes—another family room and two bathrooms upstairs, a pool and huge entertainment area out back, and six bedrooms including the delightful master bedroom downstairs. Complete with *en suite*, walk-through robe, and cosy parents' retreat, the master bedroom alone was almost as big as her Melbourne apartment!

And on her adventures she had found her

luggage and Heath's all snuggled up together on the floor of the parents' retreat. She had baulked in that moment, wondering what he had meant by it, but then she had decided that in the light of the wedding-ring fiasco it was likely he had put the bags down and forgotten about them.

'I picked out a nice bedroom upstairs,' she said, 'though I have put most of my clothes in your wardrobe, and some of my toiletries in your *en suite*. Just in case anyone goes snooping.'

'So long as we remember it's *all about appearances*.'

'Hmm,' she agreed.

'What would you like for dinner?' he asked after a few moments of substantial silence.

'I'll cook,' Jodie insisted.

'But you city girls can't cook, can you?' Heath asked, a reassuring smile finally lighting his eyes for the first time since he'd sat down. 'I was reading about your type in the newspaper the other week. Orange juice for breakfast. Eating out every night.'

'I'll have you know I can cook anything.'

'Words,' he said, a crooked smile tugging at the corner of his mouth. 'I think you ought to prove yourself with more than words.'

He twisted on his seat, facing her, but the gorgeous glint in his eyes was nothing compared with the glint of gold at his neck. As Heath had spun around a fine gold chain had slipped from beneath his shirt and now rested against his T-shirt, and on the chain, along with a small medallion, was his wedding ring.

Jodie must have stared for long enough that Heath had to see what the big deal was. He looked down, curled his fingers over the ring, and held it before his eyes.

'It's a St Christopher medal,' he said, so innocently thinking the medallion was that which had her so entranced. 'It was the one thing of Mum's I specifically asked for after she died. She wore it every day, and I've worn it every day since.'

He tucked the ring and medal back beneath his shirt, and then laid his hand over it for a moment as though branding it against his skin.

'While we're at the Run, and considering the amount of dirt and muck I work in on a daily basis, I thought it best to keep my wedding ring somewhere just as protected.'

'That's sensible,' was all Jodie could think to say. He was so worried about getting his wedding ring dirty he was protecting it, keeping it safe. It was all Jodie could do not to throw herself into his arms and beg him to forget her two-year deal and make the whole thing real then and there.

But when her wide eyes skittered upwards to

his, she realised he was watching her all too closely. An eloquent smile creased the corner of his wide mouth and Jodie leapt to her feet before she did anything stupid.

'So, dinner,' she said. 'I saw a pantry with an egg, some on-the-verge-of-overdue cheese, a tin of tuna and breadcrumbs. With that I think I can make you a feast the likes of which you've never known.'

'Sounds like a plan,' he said, standing to join her, towering over her, smiling down at her, giving her soft, uncertain heart perilously fanciful ideas.

She grabbed her jewellery pouch and held it to her thundering chest like a shield. And on shaky legs, she spun and headed for the kitchen without looking back.

CHAPTER NINE

AFTER another week and a half of driving back and forth between the peace of the Run and the mania of dealing with Mandy and Lisa in the city, Heath was bushed.

Every day he and Jodie spent together at the Run, Heath felt sure they were growing closer. And he was happier than he had been in ages, simply knowing she would be there with another amazing jewellery creation to show off when he returned from his days mustering his stock.

But after a tense couple of days in the Melbourne apartment learning more about her city life, and her city friends, watching her eat as much mascarpone as she could stomach, and sleeping on the lumpy couch, he wished he could just shove her into the Jeep and whisk her back home.

It hardly helped his growing aversion to the place that the intercom had just sounded heralding the arrival of Malcolm Cage from the Department of Immigration.

Heath buzzed him up, then turned to find Jodie standing like an ice sculpture in the kitchen, a tea towel wrapped several times around her hand, her already-pale skin drained of all colour. And when she looked at him, her wide green eyes were glittering with panic. When he realised she wasn't going to do so herself, he spun her to face the kitchen window, and undid the bow of the apron she had worn to keep mess off her new dress. Without protest, she raised her arms so he could tug it over her head.

It felt unbelievably intimate; especially considering this was the first time he had been within touching distance in days. Since that first night at the Run, she had been distant. Deliberately so, he was sure. He wasn't sure what he had done or said to make her that way, but he hadn't known any other way to deal with it other than to give her the space she so obviously desired.

But now was not the time for such a display. If she didn't pull herself together today and at least pretend to have some deeper connection to him than a shared address, her whole grand plan would unravel before her eyes.

Heath reached out and rubbed a hand down her arm, but when she didn't look around he clenched down on her soft skin and spun her back to face him. 'Jodie, look at me.'

Her big green eyes focussed. Barely.

'We are going to be okay. You and me. We are going to be fine. No matter what happens here today I am not going to let them take you away.'

He felt her body relax a very little bit in his arms, so he relaxed his grip to match. He had not meant to hang on so tight, but he felt a very real fear that if he didn't take care she might very well fly away.

'They would expect us to be nervous,' he said, 'no matter how we got to this point. Right?' He nodded, and kept nodding until she did the same.

Her pink tongue dashed out to wet her parched lips and he was undone. After days of walking around on tiptoes for fear of he knew not what, he couldn't hold back any longer. Before he had the chance to rationalise his decision, he pulled her into his arms and he kissed her.

Her petite body, pressed up against his, brought out the lion in him. He wrapped her up so tight, so warm, and soon the shakes subsided as with a heavenly sigh she kissed him back.

Quicker than he could keep up he was dragged deep into a kiss fraught with desperation. And passion. Her whole body melded to his from their lips to their knees. He knew she was only seeking solace for the upcoming toil they were about to face, but he took his own relief from the kiss all the same.

Before he lost himself completely, Heath pulled away but he kept a hold of her so that she didn't collapse onto his toes. He so often forgot how small she was. Someone her size only had so much energy with which to fight. He only hoped that in fighting against him all this time she hadn't lost the will to fight for herself.

A knock came at the door and Heath felt it deep within his ribs. Enfolding her hand in his, and giving it a quick squeeze, Heath opened the front door to find Scott, the girls' odd little neighbour whom he had made such a fool of himself over at the wedding reception, talking animatedly to a man in a suit with a briefcase.

'It's been—what? three years?' the man was saying. 'How the heck have you been?'

'Good, mate,' Scott said. 'All aces. But what are you doing here?'

The gentleman pointed over his shoulder, his thumb missing Heath's nose by a bare foot. 'I work in immigration now. Down from Canberra to officiate my first case of visa fraud.'

Scott looked up to see Heath and Jodie standing shoulder to shoulder and his beady eyes grew wide. Oh, no, of all the things that could go wrong, Heath blanched at the thought that this guy of all people, a guy who'd had a crush on his Jodie long before he'd come onto the scene, a guy who knew how he and Jodie had met, might do something to jeopardise this.

'You must be Malcolm Cage,' Heath said, his voice echoing in the small hallway.

Cage turned around, looking more than a little startled. He must have been all of twenty-one. Neat hair, new suit, and not a wrinkle marring his freshly shaved face. Great.

Heath had been counting on meeting someone who had been there and done that and seen it all before, who would be able to see how deeply he did care for Jodie, for her welfare, for her happiness, no matter the circumstances that had brought them together. But a kid, first time on the job, out to prove himself? That was an unknown entity.

The unknown entity cleared his throat, looked from Heath back to Scott, who was slinking back into his apartment.

'Well, nice to see you, Malcolm,' Scott said. 'Stop by for a cuppa if you have time, okay?'

Cage nodded, solemnly, and then turned to Jodie and Heath. Heath tucked Jodie's hand into the crook of his arm and led the way.

'Go on through to the lounge room,' Heath offered, feeling all asunder.

He drew Jodie into the kitchen, leaning her back against the sink out of sight. He took her face in his palms. 'How about you grab us a plate of nibbles and a tray of coffee, okay? Or tea, make us some tea. And only come on in when you are good and ready. I'll hold down the fort until then, all right?'

She nodded, her body shaking like a leaf. But she took a deep fortifying breath, licked her lips and nodded again. There she was, his Jodie, delicate as a willow but strong as an oak.

'Okay,' she said, punching the air for good measure. 'Shall do.'

More for his own benefit than hers, he planted one last, long, hard kiss on her soft lips, before turning and walking to bond with the man in the lounge, younger even than his youngest brother Caleb.

Jodie stayed in the kitchen listening to the murmur of voices in the other room, but they were too low for her to pick out any words.

When it came to the crunch, she wasn't sure she could do this. Standing up for others came to her as naturally as breathing, but standing up for herself was proving more difficult. Because she wasn't entirely sure she even deserved what she was asking for.

She shook her head to clear out the fog. She *did* deserve it. No matter the terrible things her mother had called her over the years, this was her chance to negate all of that, to prove that she *was* worthwhile, and vital, and deserving.

So, tea. Biscuits. Then answer questions. And at some stage that afternoon, it *would* end.

Malcolm Cage was bent over a form of some sort when she took her tray into the lounge room. She peeked over his shoulder as she passed to see if she could get a heads-up on any questions he might have.

Mr Cage sat back in his chair so suddenly his head knocked the tray and sent the tea sloshing over the sides of the pot.

'Oh, hell, I'm sorry. So sorry.' She bit her lip to stop any more profanities from spilling out.

'No worries,' Mr Cage said, running a hand over the back of his skull all the same.

Jodie managed to stop a total catastrophe from occurring by skidding around the couch and placing the tray onto the coffee-table before any more damage was done.

'Tea?' she asked their guest.

'White, no sugar, please,' Mr Cage said. She made Heath's coffee without asking how. He winked at her and she relaxed a very little. Once done, she tucked her skirt beneath her and sat next to Heath on the couch.

Mr Cage put the form from his lap onto the coffee-table and she saw it was just their marriage certificate. So much for her peeking.

Mr Cage took a sip, then opened his folder, clicked his pen and looked to the two of them with his most officious expression. 'Now,' he said, 'it's all quite straightforward. To be eligible for a Temporary Spouse Visa we have to establish several points. You must be legally married to your spouse. You must show that you and your spouse have a mutual commitment to a shared life as husband and wife to the exclusion of all others. You must show that you have a genuine and continuing relationship with your spouse, that you and your spouse are living together, and you must meet health and character requirements. And if all goes well, you must then be in Australia when the Temporary Spouse Visa is granted. Shall we begin?'

Heath nodded but Jodie found her nerves in such a tight knot she could barely remember how to focus, much less nod. *Heath Connor Jameson,* she repeated in her head, *born October eighth, second of seven children, loves all things sweet…*

'So,' Mr Cage said, 'tell me about the first moment you knew you were in love.'

Jodie's inner chanting stumbled to a breathless halt. She hadn't practised her response to a question like that. Before she could faint, or collapse or do something equally dramatic in order to distract Mr Cage, Heath was talking.

'For me it was at the end of our first night together,' he said, and Jodie turned to stare at him in mute shock. 'After a quick drink, we took a walk through the city. For hours. And I was trying my best to hide the fact that I was utterly starving. First date, you now, you want to be cool.'

Mr Cage nodded profusely, and then cleared his throat. 'Go on.'

'At about two a.m., this one spotted a kebab van. The speed with which she crossed the road to get to that kebab clinched it for me. With every extra ingredient she ordered I realised more and more that this was the woman I wanted to spend my life with.'

Mr Cage wrote copious notes for a few seconds after Heath had finished talking, and then he looked at Jodie expectantly. Heath had done his part, now there was nobody left to help her but herself. She took a shallow breath and flipped through every memory she had with Heath to find a moment where it might have believably happened. But rather than coming up blank, the moment rose to the surface with ease.

'It took me a little longer, I'm afraid. Perhaps eight hours longer,' she said, barely recognising her own confident voice. But it was a gift borne of years of dealing with doctors and lawyers determined to lock her mum away. 'My sister Louise was staying with me, and she had a family emergency, and though we had only met the day before, and Heath had somewhere else important to be, he insisted on driving us to the airport so I could spend quality time with Lou before she went home to London. In that moment I knew he was a keeper.'

She looked to Heath, the amazement at what he had done for her that day flowing over her again. He had proposed to her then and in the shadow of his heroics she had been unable to say no. She smiled tentatively and he smiled back, and her stomach dropped away into her knees.

And in that moment she knew.

She wasn't telling tales in order to have some stranger believe in her.

She loved Heath.

She hadn't been able to resist falling for his charm, his kindness, and his desire to look out for her. And the very fact that he didn't expect her to take care of him in return made her want to give him such care as was hers to give.

As Mr Cage wrote furiously on his notepad she slid a hand onto Heath's knee. He placed his hand over hers. And even though they had company, and even though only their hands were touching, it felt like the most intimate moment she had ever known.

Everything was going to be okay. In fact it was going to be better than okay. It was going to be better than she had ever thought possible. Her nerve endings zinged as her mind whirled through what her future now held with this new knowledge to guide her.

She struggled to contain the pure and unexpected joy she was feeling at the possibilities. This could be real. And not only could it be real, she wanted it to be so.

'Right,' Mr Cage said. 'So, moving on.'

Jodie turned back to him with a beatific smile lighting her face. *Bring it on,* she thought, for nothing he could ask or say could be more terrifying or enlightening as that last question.

'Okay,' Mr Cage drawled. 'Next, why don't you tell me about the website www.ahusbandina-hurry.com?'

Mr Cage looked back up at her as though he had just asked what Heath's favourite colour was. And all of Jodie's high hopes died a death in that second, as she had no idea.

Heath felt Jodie stiffen beside him. *Not now,* he thought, *not when we have come this far.*

It was almost laughable how certain he had been he could pull this off. He wanted to be married to this woman. Every strange new day in her company he knew it. He cared for her. And though, being a straight-down-the-line Australian male, he hadn't quite found the right time or the right way to tell her, he was willing to tell a stranger the depth of his need if that was what it took to keep her. What he hadn't counted on was his brave little Jodie's complete meltdown at the last post.

She was stiff and shaking all at once. Her light freckles stood out stark against her too-pale face. It seemed that the time had come for Heath to come to her rescue, whether she wanted him to or not. And it would take some fancy footwork.

Okay, he thought. *Here goes nothing.*

'My sister actually found that website,' Heath began. 'The second she saw Jodie, she thought she looked just my type. And it turned out she was right.'

'And why would your sister have been looking at such a website?' Malcolm asked, his face showing exactly how far he believed his story, true though it was.

'I have spent a lifetime working for my family with little thought for my own future, so my sisters have often taken it upon themselves to try to set me up. And though time and again they had bombed out, with this little chook, Elena could not have been more right.'

He squeezed Jodie's hand, and, drawing her startled gaze to his, he spoke directly to her.

'A fondness for redheads and those beautiful green eyes of hers got me to the first meeting, but the fact that she is brave, kind, loyal, tenacious and the sweetest, most selfless woman I have ever met got me to the altar. Now every time I look at her it kills me that she picked me.'

Once Heath finished his spiel, the room grew silent. Not even Malcolm's hyperactive pen made a move. Jodie blinked, and Heath was certain she had tears in her eyes. So long as she kept herself together.

'So how about you?' Heath asked, dragging his gaze back to Malcolm, with the intention of cutting the man's uncertainty off at the knees once and for all. 'Married? Got a girlfriend?'

'Engaged,' Malcolm admitted with his head now lowered again to his notebook.

'And how did you guys meet?' *Come on, buddy,* he begged. *Go with me. Just don't ask why Jodie was there in the first place and we're home and hosed.*

'Blind date. With her friend, actually,' Malcolm said, his mouth quirking into a smile. 'The friend took Andrea along as a chaperon in case the date didn't work out. The friend and I never stood a chance. But Andrea and I have been together ever since.'

'Well, there you go,' Heath said, slapping him on the back. 'It never seems that we marry our college girlfriends these days, do we?' He gave Malcolm his most chummy grin and was relieved when Malcolm grinned back. 'There we once were, two single guys looking for love in all the wrong places and then one day...' Heath left the sentence hanging for Malcolm to jump right on in.

And jump Malcolm did. 'And then one day. Boom. There she is.'

Malcolm looked to Jodie with big cow eyes, and Heath had little choice but to follow suit. Jodie was watching him as though he had landed in her apartment from outer space. But on that count the kid in the expensive new suit knew what he was talking about.

Boom. There she is...

'Right, now that's clear,' Malcolm said, coming over very officious all of a sudden, and Heath could have slapped himself for losing his way in Jodie's dazzling green eyes.

'I would like to speak to you one at a time now,' Malcolm said. 'Is there somewhere you can hide out, Mr Jameson, for an hour or so while I talk to your wife?'

'Right. Sure. I think I might go for a walk.'

'That's fine,' Malcolm said, swishing his hand as though the further away, the better.

Heath shuffled forward on the chair, readying himself to leave Jodie alone with the enemy, but she was clamping onto him so tight. So very tight. He leaned over and kissed her on the forehead.

'You'll do fine,' he whispered against her ear, giving her every lick of confidence he could. 'It'll all be over before you know it.'

Heath had no choice but to pick up his unsteady legs and leave, hoping against hope Jodie's determination would shine through.

An hour and a half later, Jodie found herself standing outside a French pastry shop in Acland Street staring blindly at the glass-fronted windows while Heath remained at the apartment answering Mr Cage's list of much more sensible questions.

She knew his birth date. She knew his shoe size. She knew that he loved chocolate more than life itself but that he would never eat it just before bed for fear it would give him nightmares. What she hadn't known was the moment she had fallen in love with him, until Malcolm Cage had forced her to look deep down inside herself to find out.

She loved Heath. Damn it! How had she let that happen? The stretch of time since it had occurred to her had tempered her original elation somewhat. Because it all came swimming back to her that when she loved, she loved with her heart and soul. She was ridiculously loyal to the point of putting her own interests so far down the list as to be non-existent.

And it was too soon in her project of emotional development to become so intrinsically linked with another person. It was just too soon.

She had spent so much of her life being told, 'Oh, you're Patricia Simpson's daughter,' by her mother's mad friends, by doctors, lawyers, social workers, that she had wondered whether she ought to officially change her name. Now this was her time to be just Jodie. Not someone's girlfriend, or lover, or other half. A whole person by her own right. How could she do that by falling in love? Weren't the two things mutually exclusive?

Her foot tapped against the pavement as a waitress slid a fresh, shining chocolate éclair from the back of the shelf. Her heart rate doubled as the éclair slid into a brown paper bag. And her saliva glands went into overdrive as someone else tucked the bag under their arm and paid a pittance for the pleasure they were about to imbibe.

Feeling all semblance of her will-power slip-sliding away, Jodie turned on her heel and headed on the long walk back to the apartment building, promising herself a cup of burning hot, black, un-sweetened tea when she arrived.

CHAPTER TEN

THAT night, they drove back to Jamesons Run in virtual silence. Heath hummed along with the soft songs playing on the radio while Jodie revelled in the guilty pleasure of enjoying this little intimacy.

She didn't want to talk about the interview with Malcolm Cage, and Heath made no move to either. It felt too soon. Too raw. Too fraught with the possibility that one or both of them had made some sort of glaring error that would lead to Jodie being hauled away in handcuffs. Or maybe it was the fact that things had been admitted, and, no matter how determined she was to live separately from Heath, those things were out there now.

They turned into the driveway, bumping over the now familiar cattle-grid, and Jodie felt a huge weight lift off her shoulders, as if all her trivial problems had been left back in the city. At Jamesons Run there would be no traffic jams, or road rage, or even crazy housemates coming and going at all hours of the night loaded with tequila or dodgy boyfriends or pointed questions about what the two of them got up to on the farm.

At the Run there was only peace, and quiet, and Heath.

Heath led her up the now-familiar front steps of his beautiful home, and Jodie's heart felt abnormally light. He stopped to unlock the front door, and when he shot her a quick look his usually sparkling eyes were calm.

Jodie sent him a soft smile. He smiled back, that sexy, lopsided, just-the-one-crease smile that usually sent her untested heart racing. But after the strange day they'd had, it seemed her heart was ready for anything.

They walked in the front door, side by side, and into the lounge room to find a half-dozen pale yellow lamps glowing on every spare surface giving the large room a snug welcoming feeling and—

'Cameron!' Heath's feet slammed to a halt as he looked from his brother to Jodie and back again. 'What the heck are you doing here, mate?'

Cameron looked up from his seat on the couch, his eyes hollow. 'Hey, Heath,' he said.

Heath saw the several slow seconds it took for Cameron to realise who Jodie was. Cameron stood, and Heath cringed when he saw how skinny his robust brother had become. Heath knew he had been avoiding his brother for far too long.

'You must be Jodie,' Cameron said. 'Sorry to intrude. I thought I might pop by and have dinner or something.'

Pop by? Cameron lived two hours away by car. This was more than a pop by. It had been several weeks since the funeral, and wedding preparation had been a darned good excuse for not spending time with his mourning brother. There were too many issues that he really didn't want to be thinking about, so he had gone about not thinking about them, or Cameron, to save himself the misery.

When had he become such a bastard? When had he become the sort of man to run from family the first time they really needed him? Not for money or advice, but for real help. Taking his own life by the scruff of the neck did *not* absolve him from taking part in his family's lives.

'Heath,' Jodie whispered from somewhere behind him, her voice filled with uncertainty. His heart tore at the thought that even she, who had never met the guy, could see the pain in Cameron's eyes. He held out a hand to her, halting her where she was.

'Where are the kids, Cam?' Heath asked, doing his all to keep his voice calm as he slowly eased their bags off his shoulder onto the lounge-room floor.

Cameron waved a hand in the direction of the front door. 'With Elena. She insisted I not drive so I caught a cab. Cost more than I remember it used to cost. But I guess it's been a few years since I lived out this way.'

Heath released a breath he didn't even know he had been holding. Though he was obviously not himself, at least Cameron hadn't done anything stupid with the girls.

Heath felt Jodie's small hand clasp gently around his forearm. 'How about you stay here and have a chat while I get dinner started?' she said softly.

Heath nodded. 'Thanks, Jodie. And sorry.'

Sorry my brother appeared and put a stop to...what? Something, that was for sure. Heath had known that when they got here the two of them would be finding themselves embroiled in something big. After their little chat with Malcolm Cage, Pandora's box had been opened. But now he had to put the lid back on.

Jodie gave his arm a light squeeze, then headed into the lounge. 'Sit down, Cameron. Please, don't get up for me. I'm practically a sister now, though what you need with another when you have four already I have no idea.'

She put a hand on Cameron's shoulder and gently pressed him back into the couch. He smiled up at her like a sick man who had been told his painkillers were on the way.

'How does steak and three veg sound?' she asked.

'Great,' Cameron said, his shoulders relaxing. 'Perfect.'

'Right,' Jodie said, shooting Heath a look that told him to hurry up and take over. 'I'll make you both a nice strong pot of tea, English style, and then dinner will follow close on its heels.'

And then she was gone and Heath was left alone in the quiet room with his poor dear brother, and enough memories, guilt, and age-long recriminations to drown a grown man.

Once Jodie reached the kitchen, she leant against the sink, letting the cool of the metal ease her hot palms.

Poor Cameron. She barely knew the man but she could see he was in a bad way. All of the Jameson family were robust and strong, all tall, all ridiculously healthy, and all unfairly attractive. But at best Cameron looked terribly tattered around the edges.

Cameron. Heath's brother. And Marissa's husband.

The tension between the two of them was intense. And not new. Were his family aware of it? Did they know what it was all about? Because in the moment that Cameron had looked past Heath and seen her, she had understood it all.

How stupid could she have been not to have seen it earlier? The inciting incident, the lightning bolt that had sent Heath running to the altar had been the death of Marissa. She could still hear the echo of grief in Heath's words when he'd admitted as much to her way back at the beginning.

But silly her, when he had said Marissa was an old friend he had known in college, she had assumed he meant 'friend'. Heath had joked with Malcolm Cage about not marrying his college girlfriend, and he had told her that Marissa and Cameron had overcome criticism to be together. And when Marissa died, out Heath went and married the first woman he met.

Not because he was all lonely out on his big farm, and not because he had been looking to shake things up in his life, and not because he had to find out what mascarpone was.

Jodie swallowed down the sudden bitter taste in her mouth as she finally realised Heath's real motive for marrying her. She was a blocking mechanism for his loss. He had married her *because* she was adamant she had no real designs on him emotionally, as emotionally he had nothing to give.

Oh, why now? she thought, then dug her fingernails into the unforgiving metal until they hurt. Why did this all have to blow up now, right when for the first time in her life she had thought herself ready to risk losing herself and losing her heart?

But remembering the look in Cameron's eye when she had promised tea, she knew now was not the time to be selfish. If only she had picked up that one trait from her mother, then she would have been able to move on with her life long before now and she wouldn't have found herself in the middle of such a grand mess.

Jodie made as much noise as she could while making the tea to give the men in the room next door the illusion that all was cheery.

Tea had always done that at home, given a sense of normalcy to any occasion. Social workers banging on your door? Make tea. A doctor come to deliver bad news? Make tea. Tea had served her ably over the years and she had the feeling this was going to be one of those nights where its healing powers would be needed for old and new wounds alike.

Heath wiped damp hands down the sides of his jeans as he took the five long steps to his brother's side. He sat at the very edge of the long couch, but close enough so he could reach out and give Cameron's shoulder a brotherly squeeze.

'How have you been, buddy?'

'Good,' Cameron said, nodding, though Heath could tell he could barely keep his head up.

'I'm sorry I haven't been around more. But with Jodie and the wedding and everything.' Heath knew it sounded pathetic, even to his own ears.

Cameron stopped nodding and buried his taut face in his palms. And then his body began to shake. Heath sat still as a statue as his confident, swaggering, I-can-do-anything-better-than-you brother fell apart.

He looked to the kitchen where he could hear Jodie making noises with the kettle and the like. But though he knew in his heart Jodie would know the right thing to do, the right thing to say, he couldn't call on her. He had promised he would never ask her to look out for his concerns, and he had no intention of breaking it or any other promise he had made to her.

'I shouldn't have come,' Cameron said with a muffled voice. 'I didn't realise *she* would be here. Elena said you were dividing your time between Melbourne and the Run, and Elena made it seem like for some reason *she* would stay there.' He lifted his head, ran two thin hands down his face, wiping away the dampness but not wiping away the sadness.

'She's fine, Cam. Anything you have to say you can say in front of her. Jodie's good people.'

'But it's Jodie I've come to talk to you about.'

'What about her?' Heath asked, his hackles rising instantaneously. He drew his hand back into his lap.

Cameron sniffed, fortifying himself and shaking out his recent crying jag. Then he turned to Heath, his face a mask of pain. 'I want you to tell me, to my face, that you have not married this woman as some sort of emotional flinch against Marissa's death.'

Suddenly Heath's hackles were not his biggest problem. As he looked into his brother's blue eyes, a paler version of his own, he was taken aback that Cameron had had the capacity to come up with such an idea. But above and beyond he felt a deep-seated need to protect the woman at the centre of their conversation.

'Watch yourself, Cam,' Heath warned, doing his best to keep his palms from turning into fists.

'It's not such a stretch, Heath. Elena told me that you only met this girl some time after the funeral, which means you can't have known her more than a month before you married her. I know she is some sort of unemployed tourist. She might have found you at a low point and taken advantage, using you to stay here, or to get to the family money. How well can you really know her in such a short space of time?'

Cameron was half so very wrong, and half so very right that Heath had no idea how to answer him. 'She has not taken advantage of me in any way, shape or form, Cameron,' he eventually said, 'and I thank you not to say such a thing aloud ever again. Not in my house, and not in my hearing, or I just don't know what I might do.'

But in his state, Cameron was not to be deterred. 'So why haven't you married before now? Why marry the instant Marissa is finally out of reach for good?'

Heath was shocked by the bitterness in Cameron's voice. He had never let on to Cameron how hurt he had been when he and Marissa had declared their intention to marry, but he must have sensed it all the same. But his melancholy had stemmed more from the fact that his favourite brother was growing up and moving away, leaving him alone to the fate that had been thrust upon him.

Had Cameron been holding onto the fear that his big brother might come a-calling, for all these years? Wow. He had. Heath saw it in Cameron's face. In his stiff body. In his red eyes. All these years Cameron had half been expecting Heath to blow his lid and take Marissa back. Beside the fact that Marissa would not have had him, it had never once occurred to Heath to even try.

He'd had a fondness for Marissa, she had been a lovely woman, but she'd had no gumption. No guts. Not like his Jodie. He had never known anyone so plucky. She had more energy and determination in her little finger than could be found in Marissa or a hundred like her.

But Heath also knew that there was no way he could say all that to his brother. Heath had been fond of Marissa, had been in a way envious of the steadfast relationship she'd had with his brother, but Cameron had *loved* her.

Cameron had lost her in a most tragic way, whereas Heath had merely been dumped. And he knew now he should have thanked her for it a long time ago. He ought to have thanked her for making his brother so happy on her wedding day when she had thanked him for being such a good friend. Some friend he was.

But maybe now was the time to do so, time to thank the one person left to whom it obviously mattered most.

Once the tea was ready, Jodie put her ear to the door to make sure the time was right. There was no way she wanted to walk into the middle of something personal. She pushed the swing door open a fraction and strained her ear to make sure.

'Do you really think after all these years that I am still in love with Marissa?' she heard Heath say and she hiccuped in a shocked breath, which she then followed quickly with a hand slapped across her mouth.

'I really do. Tell me the truth, Heath,' Cameron returned. 'I will know if you don't.'

There was a pause. A pause that felt as if it lasted a thousand years, as Jodie dared not take breath again until one of the men made a noise. But when she felt another hiccup threatening, she let the door slide shut without making a whisper of noise.

She hiccuped wretchedly on her way back to the island bench and leant against it for fear she might slide to the ground. The tray of tea with its fine china cups laughed up at her. Soothing? Calming? Fix-all? She fought the urge to wipe the whole bloody lot off the bench and smash it to the floor.

Instead she grabbed the phone off the kitchen wall and dialled in Mandy's mobile number.

'Cameron,' Heath said, 'would I have stayed, running this place for so long after Mum and Dad died, if I didn't feel that way? Would I have let Marissa go if it was that important for me to have her in my life? Would you?'

'No,' Cameron said on a heavy breath. 'Neither of us would.'

Heath shuffled closer to his brother and lay a hand on the kid's shoulder. 'You loved her. And she loved you. And now she is gone you don't need to be muddying her memory. She will be missed, by all of us. But none of us will ever understand what you have gone through without going through such a loss ourselves.'

Cameron nodded, not even trying to cover up his pain. He sniffed and looked back at Heath, his fierce eyes now toned down to a more sheepish look. 'So you and this wild English rose. Are you the real thing?'

The real thing? Considering the odd circumstances of their meeting? Considering they couldn't go a day without being at loggerheads? Considering slick young Malcolm Cage of the immigration department could very well hand down an official finding saying otherwise?

He thought of her often prickly demeanor, her soft warm lips that reacted to him on such a primal level whenever they kissed, and those eyes, those great green pools of energy that lit up her small face when she was happy and gave her away the instant she wasn't.

'I don't know,' Heath said, feeling a little breathless as he let the terrifying truth escape his numb lips. 'Maybe. How did you know that Marissa was the one? How did you know she was worth the risk?'

'In the same way you know when they're not the one—you just know.' And then Cameron smiled. Not a great smile, but a definite curling of the lips, and Heath felt as though a little ray of sunshine might just have entered his brother's life for the first time in weeks.

'Yep?' Mandy answered.

'Mandy, it's Jodie.'

'Jodes! How did you go with the guy from the immigration thingy? Two thumbs up? Have you touched a cow yet?'

'Okay. Not sure. And no.'

'Found any more bedrooms hidden away in spare wings of your mansion?' Mandy asked, and Jodie could tell she was feeling mighty proud of herself. 'And did you just hiccup?'

'No. And yes. And don't expect Christmas presents from Tiffany's just yet, Mandy. I think I've made a big mistake.'

She heard Mandy's feet slide from the coffee-table and hit the floor and knew that she finally had her friend's attention. 'Why? What happened? What's wrong?'

Before I even realised he had the power to do

so, he's gone and broken my heart, she thought, rubbing at her aching temple. 'Did you ever wonder why he married me, Mandy?'

'Well…'

'Come on. You must have. He's beautiful. And generous. And rich as Midas I found out when he showed me his bank statement before our interview today. Didn't you think there had to be some big secret hidden reason why a guy like that couldn't find a wife by normal means by now?'

'Okay, I wondered. Lisa, Louise and I talked about it a bit. But you seemed so sure and we didn't want to worry you. Is he…did he lose his old fella in some sort of farm-related accident?'

'No! Well, I wouldn't know actually as we haven't…we won't be…oh, Mandy, it's much more sordid and excruciating than that.'

'Is that possible?'

Jodie should have realised Mandy would likely think there could be nothing worse. 'I think he married me in order to dull the pain of losing the woman he really loved.'

The end of the line went silent for a few moments before Mandy's voice came back, low and doubtful. 'And who might that be?'

'His brother's dead wife.' As soon as she said the words Jodie's heart clenched so hard in her chest she could barely breathe.

After a lengthy pause Mandy asked, 'Are you sure you aren't getting your life mixed up with an episode of Lou's *Beach Street*?'

'Mandy—'

'Jodie! Heath is prime-cut meat. And of all the women in all the world he could have chosen to marry for whatever deranged reasons you may think he has, he chose you. So jump the guy, for goodness' sake, while he's yours for the taking. And if it turns out I was right after all, let me know—I have twenty bucks riding on it.'

Jodie's hiccups vanished as she choked on the response she wished to give to that remark.

'Jodie, I'm kidding. Well, I'm not kidding about the twenty. But come on. Not one of us came up with that as motive. We were there at the wedding. We saw the way he looked at you all day. We saw the kiss. Or kisses. The odds on you guys lasting doubled that night and have gone up pretty steadily ever since.'

'How many of you have a bet going?'

'Me, Lisa, Jake, Scott, the handsome cab driver from your wedding, half the wait staff at The Cave. I rang Louise the other night to see if she wants in but she refused on principle, though I reckon she could have made herself a tidy fortune as it's looking like her guess will come up trumps in the end—'

'Goodbye, Mandy,' she said and this time she hung up. Maybe Mandy was right. Maybe one of the other hundred odd people out there rooting for her was right.

Only time would tell. And out here in the middle of nowhere, time was all she had.

Cameron reached out and gave Heath a slap on the back. 'Right. Well, I think I've stayed long enough. Especially if you and Jodie are *maybe* for real. I'll head back to Elena's for the night.'

Cameron stood, and Heath with him.

'Stay,' Heath said. 'You know there's plenty of room.'

'Nah, I really ought to get back to the kids.'

'Right. But don't catch a cab. Take the Jeep. I'll be fine with just the ute. We're planning on staying here until Christmas Day as it is. Get Elena to bring it back then, all right?'

Cameron nodded and headed for the door.

Heath glanced at the kitchen, which had been eerily quiet for some time. But he thought it best to get Cameron home while he was on an even keel. His brother and his wife could get to know one another better over a pot of tea another time.

If he had his way, they had all the time in the world.

* * *

Jodie steeled herself, grabbed the tray, and, without making the mistake of listening at the door again, she pushed her way out into the great room.

But no one was there. When she heard the front door close, she put the tray on the coffee-table and waited for one or both men to return. Heath came in, head down, face clouded with all sorts of emotions.

'Has Cameron gone?' she asked.

Heath looked up and took a second to really see her. Boy, did she wish that she had been able to hear the end of that conversation.

He ran a hand over his face, then across the back of his neck. 'Yeah, he's gone back to Elena's for the night.'

'He didn't have to go,' she insisted.

'Yeah,' Heath said, watching her carefully through his charged eyes. 'Yeah, he did.'

He moved to the couch, sat, and patted the seat beside him. She joined him on a patch of comfort-able red leather.

Heath poured the tea. 'Black, no sugar, right?'

'Thank goodness you're a quick learner,' she said.

His brow furrowed for a moment before he blinked away whatever he was thinking.

She drank the now-lukewarm tea in one gulp, then, feeling in dire need of a long soak in a tub to wash away her confusion, Jodie made a move to stand, but Heath stopped her with the touch of his hand on her arm.

'Why do you really want to stay here so badly, Jodie?'

Jodie sat back, her pulse picking up pace at Heath's intimate touch. She bit her lip to stop herself from thinking that way. 'I love Australia.'

Heath shook his head, and watched her over the top of his tea. 'There's more to it than that. What was so bad about going back to London? I always thought the Beefeaters looked a little odd, but enough so for you never to set foot on British soil again?'

Jodie couldn't bring herself to laugh at his half-hearted joke. She just continued staring at her hands in her lap.

'Are you running from the law?' Heath finally asked.

Now that brought a smile to Jodie's face, until she noticed that Heath was dead serious. 'Have you been thinking that in the back of your head all this time? That I am some sort of criminal, on the run, skipping town before the cops had the chance to run my prints?'

Heath shrugged. 'Not really. Not all this time. Just every now and then it has been one of the possibilities tracking through my mind.'

'And what do you think I might have done?

Robbery? Murder? Bio-terrorism?' And *still* he married her!

He raised one blond eyebrow. 'You tell me.'

She spun to face him down. 'I am not on the run from the law, okay?'

'Okay.'

Feeling as if she had dodged a bullet, Jodie went to make her move but was stopped again, this time by Heath's hand on her thigh. And with that touch searing through her dress she could not have moved from the couch if the house were burning down around her.

'So why? Why move to Australia, and why after ten-odd months decide that you simply had to stay, at the cost of leaving behind everything you have ever known without a backward glance?'

His voice was calm, but she could feel intensity curled deep within him like a jungle cat ready to pounce. And she knew that there was more to his question than—why Australia? It was the big one. Why not London?

She knew she wasn't getting out of this one. Not with misdirection, or an argument, or smoke and mirrors. He had asked her a reasonable question and the time had come to say the answer out loud.

She blew out a long slow breath, collected her thoughts and said, 'It's my mum.'

'What's she like?' he encouraged, kindly allowing her to dip her toes in the water of disclosure.

'She doesn't look much like me. She's taller, her hair is fiery red, her legs are to die for, and her personality... Well, let's just say that if she was in this room now you would forget I was here within five minutes.'

'I doubt that very much,' he said. His hand moved to rest upon her knee and his thumb began gently circling her kneecap.

'I'm serious. She is dramatic, to say the least. Add to that a veritable cocktail of mental and emotional ailments that can only be kept in check by a rigorous combination of medication, psychological massage, and around-the-clock care, she is...difficult to live with. And since we did not have the funds to pay for proper care anywhere else, it fell on my shoulders.'

'You took care of her all by yourself?'

'Pretty much every day since I was thirteen years old,' she said, doing her all to keep her mind off the warmth reverberating from his gentle touch.

'Did she appreciate what you did for her?'

Jodie's cheek twitched as she remembered the years of verbal and emotional abuse that had been her mother's version of thanks. But then she visualised their yearly Christmas shopping sprees through Chelsea and was able to find a kind of emotional balance.

'Not so much,' she admitted. 'Which is one reason why I am so very glad that she now has Derek—a darling retiree who thinks the sun rises and sets with her. They have been together a little over a year, and so far everything is rosy. But the minute his patience or the money runs out…'

'You think she'll want you back?' he asked.

'Every time the phone rings.'

His hand moved higher, infinitesimally so, but Jodie could tell. The simple circular movements of the pads of his fingers merely lulled her further and further under his spell.

'So you married me,' he said, 'in order to anchor yourself here. To give yourself a solid reason not to go back.'

She nodded, though perhaps she was just trembling.

'I can't believe that you would find it that hard to say no to her. You've said no to me any number of times and I don't think it caused you even a blip of remorse.'

'She's a very hard woman to deny,' she said, her voice huskier than normal. 'She's a fireball, an electric spark, a bundle of energy and I'm…'

What? Terms her mother had used over the years came back to her like slaps across the face.

*A wet sponge? A mouse? Not worth the money she
spent on food and clothes?*

'I'm more regular,' she eventually said.

'Regular?' Heath repeated. 'Jodie, sweetheart,
the last adjective I would ever attribute to you
would be *regular*.'

His hand moved away from her knee and she
all but whimpered. But when he reached out and
took a clump of her waves into his fist, running
his fingers slowly down the length and watching
as each hair slid from his gentle grasp, the
whimper faded to nothing. Jodie's breathing es-
calated, her chest rising and falling with each
continuing second of his intimate but not-inti-
mate-enough touch.

'I have no idea what sort of woman your
mother is, but you, my sweet wife, are luminous,'
he said, his eyes swinging back to hers, their blue
depths darkening with something that to her
seemed a heck of a lot like desire.

'You are delightful, for ever surprising, and
compassionate, and yet you have a temper which
I never see coming. And I've recently decided I
like it that way.'

So if he thought all of those things, if she kept
him intrigued and in laughter and on the edge of
his seat, then was there any possible way she
could make him forget Marissa once and for all?

But even if she could, would it be worth it if she were for ever second best? She wished she could just come out and ask him. The words caused a sour taste beneath her tongue and she knew that if she didn't find out now, she never would.

'Heath,' she said, her soft voice an echo of the difficulty she had in summoning her words.

'Jodie,' he said back, his eyes following the track of his hand through her curls.

'Did you marry me to get over Marissa once and for all?'

His hand stopped its heavenly path and his eyes snapped straight to hers. And if she thought her heart had been running a race earlier she'd had no idea. Confronted with such intensity in his big blue eyes, her heart all but galloped from her chest.

Finally he sat back with a ragged sigh and she felt a wave of cool air take up the space where he had just been.

'This is fast becoming the strangest day of my life.' He ran a ragged hand through his hair. 'If I didn't know better I would think you have all gathered for some secret meeting without me. Where on earth did *you* get that idea?'

'I put two and two together. From things you've said.' She took a deep breath and dived into the deep end. 'But mostly from overhearing your conversation with Cameron just now.'

His eyes slid her way, and then towards the front door through which his brother had recently departed, and then back to her, careful, wary, unsure. 'How much did you overhear?' he asked.

Oh, now she'd done it. How could she possibly say without giving herself away? Without telling him why she needed to know? 'Why don't you just tell me what you said?'

He blinked, and she was sure his eyes were actually lit with laughter. But he admitted nothing.

'Why did you want to marry me, Heath?' she asked, her innumerable frustrations getting the better of her. 'What's in it for you? I've changed my mind on your motivation a dozen times already, but now I just can't see what *you* could possibly gain from this unless it is respite from a broken heart.'

'Companionship,' he said, all too quickly, and Jodie just knew that wasn't the whole truth. 'Marissa's death did come into it. It showed me how alone I am out here.'

'Okay, but at the end of our two years do you plan to go through it all again? Find some other woman after Australian citizenship that you can bring out here and introduce to your family and welcome into your home?'

Her voice was growing overly loud; she could see Heath flinching from her accusations. Well, that was just tough.

'Sure. Why not?' he said, folding his arms and glaring back at her. 'My life was just too comfortable before you came along. What I really needed to do to spice up my life was to sleep on a lumpy couch three nights out of seven, start wearing pyjamas to bed so as not to scare my half-dozen housemates in the morning, and have some kid fresh out of college questioning me about my sexual habits on his first day on the job.'

That *so* wasn't the answer she had been looking for.

'Do you really think that I would agree to go through all this junk, for you, just because I am pining over another woman?'

Absolutely unwilling to let him make this about her, she threw her arms in the air. 'Fine. If you won't answer me directly then I guess that means I can go on believing what I will. Goodnight, Heath.' She turned and headed for the stairs up to her bedroom.

'Why are you always running, Jodie?' Heath asked.

Jodie's feet stopped. It took all her strength to stop them, but stop them she did. She even gathered enough strength to turn and glower. 'Excuse me?'

Heath was standing, glaring back at her from the middle of the lounge room. 'You have run away from home. And now you are trying to run away from me. I'm not such a pushover I am going to let that happen without a fight.'

'You want me to fight?' she asked. 'I have spent my life fighting. Fighting to protect my mum from confinement, from doing herself harm, from doing me harm. But now I am here, I had hoped I had finally found a place where I could allow things to happen more naturally. Fighting is the last thing I want.'

He came to her, taking her arms in his strong hands, forcing her to look at him. To really see him.

'Then stop.' His eyes blazed down at her, filled with a passion she couldn't even begin to decipher. 'Stop fighting me. Stop fighting this. Stop looking for reasons why this can't work. You won't regret it, I promise. I won't let you.'

'I…I don't think I know how to stop.'

His face softened further until he almost smiled. She was so close to him she could see the myriad blues in his irises, the old scar in his eyebrow, and the varied colours in his golden skin. This was a face that had lived. And loved.

And lost. But the emotion she saw now above all others was hope.

'Help me,' she said, uttering two words that in her whole young life she had struggled hard not to think, much less say aloud. But she wanted what he was offering her, more than she wanted anything else. 'Help me learn to stop fighting.'

And then, with a growl as primal as the sunbaked land surrounding their outback oasis, he kissed her. Sweeping her into his arms with such compulsion it was as though he had been waiting weeks for her to say the word.

Before she even realised that she had been lifted off the floor, Heath was laying her back onto his bed with a gentleness that belied the desire in his eyes, and the heat in his kiss.

At the last moment he hesitated.

But he was right, she would not regret this. No matter his motives, or hers, no matter if Malcolm Cage whipped her dream out from under her, no matter if in two years' time Heath did let her go, or she let him go, she would never regret this.

So she reached out to him, burying her hands into his soft hair and drawing his mouth to hers.

CHAPTER ELEVEN

HEATH sat upon the window-seat in his bedroom, staring out at the moonlit expanse. Even as Jodie lay naked in his bed, he could still scarcely believe that they had made love. It had been building for so long, but he had still believed her to be out of his reach. Now that the storm had broken it only made him ache for her all the more. His desire for her was unquenched, and, in his lifetime, unmatched.

The shuffling of fresh cotton behind him got his attention. He turned to find Jodie stretching beneath his sheets. She rolled to face him, waking for a moment, her lovely face curling into a soft smile before her eyes slid closed once more. He could have sat there and watched her all night.

He only wished he could turn back the clock to when she had asked him about Marissa, for he had known the instant the words left her mouth that her question had not been about Marissa at all. But when she had been brave enough to ask how he truly felt about her, he had taken the coward's way out and shown her instead.

Sure, he had made progress with Cameron earlier the night before, talking through his feelings. That had been a big step for him, ground-breaking, really, for a country boy who had spent a lifetime being strong and steadfast for everyone else while keeping his own dilemmas buried down deep within himself. But this next step would be harder still. The hardest thing he would ever do in his life.

To tell a woman he cared for her, while having no clue that she would or even could return his feelings, would be the biggest risk he had taken in his life. He would be risking rejection, embarrassment, and even heartbreak. She desired him. There was no doubting that now. But had her childhood made it impossible for her to give herself to someone fully? Was he merely an easy way for her to run from her problems back home?

He looked back out at the moonlit night, sending out thoughts to the gods of earth and sky to give him strength.

He uncurled himself from his seat, pulled back the soft cool cotton sheets and lay next to his wife, taking complete advantage of her sleeping state as he wound himself around her, spooning her heavenly form, hoping that the reward for his risk would be that this night would be one of many.

* * *

The next morning, Jodie made a full English breakfast. Her life had gone way past the sort of drama that a cup of tea could fix. Grease, fat, and overcooked breakfast meats were the order of the day.

Besides which, she was starving. Her stomach was hollow. For a girl whose usual weekly exercise output was the walk to and from the tram, the day before had taken it out of her in more ways than one.

She stopped scrambling eggs for a moment and allowed herself a little daydream. If Heath didn't realise her feelings for him after that display, he was as thick as the willow trunk in his main paddock. But then again maybe she should have told him in no uncertain terms last night. In the cold light of day it could be too late. Sunlight had a way of showing up every flaw, every *faux pas*...

She set the table, tracking down crockery, cutlery, placemats, coasters and all the bits and pieces she needed to put on her spread. There was tea, coffee, juice, and anything and everything that could be considered breakfast. So when Heath came in through the laundry door, she had every angle covered.

'Good morning,' she said brightly, standing at the head of the table with the chair pulled out.

She felt the throw rug she had wrapped about herself slipping off her shoulder, so she gave it a self-conscious hitch. Even though Heath had seen and known parts of her body even she was unfamiliar with, she still felt too shy to run about the house naked.

Heath slowed, wiping dirty hands on an even dirtier rag, his eyes roving over the feast. 'What's this?'

'Full English breakfast just like you would find in any good café or pub back home.'

'Do you mind if I wash up first? The ute has been leaking oil and while you were still asleep I thought I'd take the time to have a look.'

Jodie's spirits dropped with every second that he looked anywhere but at her. She knew what he was really saying and she understood. He had woken before her, finding her naked in his arms, and he had made a run for it, finding something 'important' to do to get him out of the house so he wouldn't have to face her and the *morning after* conversation.

Well, that was fine. Just fine. There was no way Jodie needed him telling her that the night before had been a mistake. That it hadn't meant anything. She could figure it out from the signs all on her own.

'Go,' she said brightly as though nothing had

changed, 'wash up. But don't be too long or it will get cold.'

'Sure,' he said, then paused, looking at her, finally. His face softened; the expression of confusion fading away. Jodie felt herself heating under his glance. Melting. Burning up with a mixture of awkwardness and remembered passion.

Put me out of my misery, she thought. *Just tell me that you now agree with my need for abstinence and we can get on with it. I am tough. Well, I can be tough. Just be hard with me, cruel to me, negate me, and it will make me tough again.*

But when he looked at her like that with those eyes so filled with warmth, longing, and wonder she couldn't be tough. She became soft, yielding, and full of hope when for the longest time her life had not seemed destined to accommodate such feelings.

Her heart picked up pace as she was sure he was about to say something. She held her breath, not certain she was ready to hear it, whatever it was. But then with a frustrated frown he turned and stormed into the bedroom.

The second he was gone, she slumped into a chair and let her forehead land on the tabletop with a resounding thump.

Heath stripped off his oil-spattered clothes and jumped into the steaming shower, letting the water soak away the dirt, and grime, and discomfort he felt in holding his tumultuous feelings inside of him.

He'd run. He'd accused her of running the night before, yet the second he had woken to the cold, harsh light of day he had run. He hadn't woken her with a kiss to the end of her upturned nose as he had so ached to do. Years of holding his feelings in check had compelled him to swing his legs from the bed, pull on jeans and an old flannelette shirt, and sent him out to his toolbox.

Now there she was, all wrapped up in a worn old throw rug from the end of his bed, likely with nothing else underneath, her hair mussed, her face pink from sleep, having cooked him a feast. And his sturdy rider's legs had all but buckled beneath him at such an endearing sight.

She had made a peace-offering, a way of bridging their usual polite conversation and the fantastical night before. Whereas he, with his apprehensive tongue forming nothing but knots inside his mouth, had clomped through the sweet domestic scene like a bull in a china shop. Again he realised that this slip of a girl was far braver than him.

He turned off the hot water with such force his wrist hurt. Then he stood still beneath the cold shower, letting the chilly droplets spear his skin. It was all he deserved.

Time apart might be just what he and Jodie both

needed. And when he had been working on the ute, the fates had intervened in the form of Andy, his station manager. That afternoon he and the boys would be heading out on a two-night camp-out. Andy had done a headcount and a few head of cattle might have been left behind on the last muster. So Heath had put up his hand the minute Andy had told him the score.

So this simple farmer only hoped that in turning to the stars for help he could summon the words to tell his wife what she really meant to him.

A few hours later, Jodie stood on the veranda, waving as Heath, Andy and a handful of others walked their horses out towards the hills at the edge of Heath's property.

She watched them until they became specks in the distance and she was left all alone with nothing but her thoughts. But, Jodie didn't want to think any more.

So the second they were out of her sight she did an about-turn, marched into Heath's kitchen, pulled out a packet of chocolate Tim-Tams, an apple tea cake she had made for them and then 'forgotten' to pack, and a tube of condensed milk.

She marched back out to the love seat, and sat with the afternoon sunshine belting onto her face.

Without a second thought, she ripped open the biscuit packet, not caring to keep the ends neat. This was one packet that would not need to keep the remaining contents fresh.

She grabbed a thick chocolate rectangle, and bit down, her teeth sinking into the soft outer layer before crunching through the brown biscuit middle. She all but drooled as the taste exploded in her mouth. The sugar, so long missing from her system, melted against her tastebuds.

Before she had fully enjoyed the first mouthful, she slid the rest of the biscuit into her mouth until the crumbs and layers filled her cheeks and she could barely chew without spilling crumbs all over herself.

To wash down the last of the biscuit, she opened the tube of condensed milk, tipped her head back, and squeezed until she filled every inch of her mouth. The smooth texture and seriously sweet taste were so magical, so heavenly, so decadent, they almost made her cry.

It was official—she had no will-power. She had sure proved that last night with Heath. So why bother pretending in the rest of her life? She was hopeless. Just as her mother had always told her she was.

She ate and ate and ate until her stomach would hold no more, and then, with a bellyful of sugar,

and a head full of guilt, Jodie rolled up into a ball
on the love seat and cried.

A ringing land-line phone woke Jodie at around
one the next morning. Eyes half closed, she struggled to find the phone under her hastily discarded
clothes on the table next to Heath's side of the
bed.

As she sat up she realised her stomach hurt. It
hurt like nothing she had ever felt before. She
licked her dry lips to find the taste of chocolate at
the edge of her mouth and then knew why. It was
self-inflicted pain, all of it, self-medication gone
wrong, so she deserved no sympathy. And even if
she did, she was all alone, and would get none.

'Hello?' she groaned miserably into the phone.

'Jodie, doll, it's Derek.'

Now *that* woke her up quicker than any shril-
ly-ringing phone or sugar headache could. 'Oh,
my. Derek. Hello!'

'I got this number from your friend Mandy.
Hope that's all right. Is it late there? I'm never
quite sure how to figure out the time difference.'

'No, it's fine. And I asked Mandy to pass it on if
you called. I'd heard you were back in London,' she
said, caught between using her spare hand to rub
her prickly eyes or her aching tummy. 'I've
been…living in between places for a little while

now, but since you haven't had your answering machine turned on I haven't been able to let you know.'

About her move. Or about Heath. But for that news she needed to talk to her mum direct. When the usually shy and reserved Derek didn't offer to pass the phone to her mum instantly, fear created a trickle of sweat down her back.

'Is Mum there?' Jodie asked.

'Asleep,' he said, but the answer came too quickly, too nervously.

Jodie felt her stomach drop away. Patricia was asleep. Had she had an attack? An episode? An outburst? Had she been sedated? And why now? Were the fates playing tricks on her? Did Patricia know that Jodie was in the process of making a life for herself? Did she sense that she might not be coming home?

'How is she, Derek? Be honest with me. I can take it.'

'Well, she has been a little upset of late.'

Upset. Upset for most people would mean a bit of a frown. For Patricia it could mean a sit-down in the middle of a public place that could only be fixed by police intervention.

'Upset, how?'

'Well, Jodie, it is her birthday in four days, and I know that your return flight was not meant to be until just before New Year, but it would mean so much to her if you came home.'

His story just didn't feel right. Jodie looked at her watch. One in the morning, taking into account daylight savings, meant it was two in the afternoon there. 'Wake her for me, Derek. I need to talk to her now.'

She heard Derek's pause. The last thing he would wish to do would be to go against Patricia's wishes. Well, Patricia was going to have to come second for once.

'Now, Derek. It's important.'

'Well, I would, but you see I can't. She's not here; she's at the hospital.'

Jodie's aching stomach clenched so hard she thought she might be sick. Hospital? Damn it! Why hadn't they called her sooner? She had done too much to get Patricia to a stable stage in her life for it to all fall apart again.

'Okay,' she said, hearing the distress in Derek's voice. 'It's okay, Derek. Look, go to Mum. Be with her. And tell her…'

Tell her what? Tell her to snap out of it? To be the grown-up? But Jodie knew that wouldn't happen. Not like this. Not with Derek as a go-between. Not with her mother medicated up to her eyeballs.

The time had come to sort out her life once and for all. If she really wanted to move on, move ahead, move into a stage of her life where she could really be her own person, and make her own decisions and be strong enough to stick by them, to love Heath as he deserved to be loved whether she would always be second-best for him or not, and to let him know it, then she had to clear away the cobwebs of the past once and for all.

'Derek,' she said, loud and clear, making sure she had his full attention. 'Tell her I'm coming home.'

Early the next morning, Jodie took a big deep breath and called Heath's sister Elena—the one person in Heath's family that she knew was suspicious of her, even though Heath would never admit it.

'Hello? Stop that! If you don't stop that, I will come over there and…that's better. Good boy.'

'Elena? It's Jodie,' she said once there was a pause on the other end of the phone. She was preparing herself to add 'Heath's wife', when Elena spoke up.

'Jodie,' Elena repeated. 'Right. Well, hello.'

Jodie heard it in her voice. Elena knew. Elena might well have been the one to have shown Heath her website in the first place, but she wasn't at all happy about how that had turned out.

'You're calling about Christmas, I expect,' Elena said. 'There'll be those of us from the wedding and a couple of dozen extra in-laws and out-laws as well. But I don't want you to think you have to put on some big spread. The rest of the Jameson clan will bring food, and all you have to do is sit back and let us show you how we do Christmas down under. Okay?'

Christmas? Oh, no. Jodie ran her spare hand over her tired eyes. She was going to arrive in London three days before Christmas. With her mum on the verge of a spell she was preparing for the idea that she might not even be home by New Year.

Home.

She looked around the warm oak kitchen and out through the window across the red dusty plains. *This* was home. This faraway haven of peace and nature, of heat and flies, and, most of all, of Heath. This was her home.

And she was about to leave with fair certainty that she would not be able to return in the foreseeable future for fear of men in rent-a-cop uniforms refusing to stamp her passport and locking her away in some dark cold room as they questioned her for hours as they did on those TV shows all about airline security.

'This isn't about Christmas, Elena. Sorry. Heath is out on a two-night cattle run, and I need to get hold of him quite urgently.'

'Oh. Umm. He's lost his satellite-phone thingy again, has he? Did he leave you a map of where they'll be? The easiest thing would be to ride out and join them. If he's only out for two nights you'll be able to find him at a gallop within a couple of hours, I'm sure.'

'I can't ride.'

'Oh. Stop that! Right now! If I have to count to three… One…Two… Good boy. Sorry, Jodie. You can't ride? Are you okay? Do you need an ambulance? Are you hurt?'

'No, nothing like that. I never learned.' But it seemed that if she ever came back she would definitely have to learn to ride a horse. Otherwise these outback Australians would never take her for one of their own. 'Anyway, that's not the problem. It's just my mum, back home in London, she isn't well.' Understatement of the year. 'I must go back as soon as possible.'

'But what about your temp visa?' Elena said. 'I thought it hadn't come through yet.'

Her visa? Elena knew not only about how they had met but about her desire for a temporary visa? No wonder she had not warmed to her as the others had.

A clock somewhere in the huge house chimed six in the morning and Jodie felt time slipping away.

'It hasn't,' she admitted, feeling that being

forthright was the only way to win this woman over. 'But even though I would give my right leg to wish it had, I am stuck. I have to go back to London right away. And I have to let Heath know. Elena, I don't have anywhere else to turn. I need your help.'

There. She had said it again. It seemed once she had jumped that hoop she could jump it again and again.

'Right,' Elena said into the loaded silence. 'Leave him a note on the hall table and he'll find it. Family tradition.'

'Thanks, Elena.'

'No worries. And I do hope we'll see you back here for Christmas.'

'From the bottom of my heart I hope so too.'

As Jodie hung up the phone she saw a swirl of dust in the distance. It was her cab. That meant she only had minutes before she had to leave. Barely enough time to write a note three lines long, much less a note that could possibly explain why she had to leave so suddenly and how much she hoped she could come straight back. To him. For two years, or for ever if he would have her.

Five minutes later, with a note propped up on the hall table, Jodie left.

In the cab she kept her eyes forward, unable to allow herself to look back, as the sight of the large house with the silver roof and the horse fences, and stables and red plains and distant hills and eucalypts fading to a speck in the rear window might very well break her heart.

CHAPTER TWELVE

TWENTY-FOUR-ODD hours later, Jodie stood shivering on the cracked pavement, looking up at the familiar red-brick block of flats as grey rain splashed down on top of her in great wet sheets.

Not for the first time in the past twenty-four hours, she wished Heath were with her, his warm, gallant hand at her back, his broad shoulder to lean on.

When she had boarded the British Airways plane the attendants with their eighties outfits and eighties haircuts had actually brought a smile to her face as they had made her think of Heath. By the time the plane had left the tarmac in Melbourne, the thought of returning to London had not frightened her nearly as much as the thought that she might not be able to come back to him.

She had phoned Jamesons Run from Heathrow but there had been no answer, and there was nothing more she could think to say on the answering machine that she had not said in her simple note.

With a grand sigh she walked the old grimy staircase up three floors, trawled the long front graffiti-covered balcony past a half-dozen other sad-looking flats and knocked on her mother's plain brown front door.

She heard noises from within. English noises. Clinking teacups. *Coronation Street* on TV. She shivered again and this time it had nothing to do with the cold.

Finally, the door opened to reveal Patricia in all her glory—hair still fire-engine red, perfumed to sneezing point, and dressed as if she were about to sing cabaret, not as if it was a winter Wednesday at home.

'Jodie! Darling!' Patricia cried out, giving Jodie great gushy air kisses.

Jodie kissed back while trying to keep her luggage from becoming squashed in the crush. When she pulled back, she had a good look at the mother she had not seen in almost twelve months. Patricia was a good deal more tanned from all her travelling, and she also looked a good deal older, smaller, and a whole lot less intimidating.

And for the briefest of seconds Jodie wondered what she had been fussing about all those months. And then Patricia became…well, Patricia.

'You've put on weight,' she said. 'Around the tummy. And you're all freckled. When did that happen?'

Jodie blinked at her mother and forced herself not to undo all the good the past year had brought her. She took a deep breath and channelled confidence from Lisa, poise from Louise, chutzpah from Mandy, and brawn from Heath.

'It happened on my year in Australia,' Jodie said in a nice loud voice. 'Well, it was not quite a year. Before rushing back here, to be with you, I had around eight days left before my visa ran out.'

She dumped her heavy bags in the hall when nobody asked to give her a hand with them.

'But how are you, Mum?' Jodie asked, watching carefully for signs of stress, overindulgence, and excessive exuberance, evidence that she hadn't been eating properly, bathing properly, and sleeping properly. 'Derek said you were at the hospital.'

'Hospital? I was out visiting Tina Smythe's new granddaughter in hospital the other day. But I am just fabulous, darling, now that you are here, and just before my birthday.' Patricia turned and pointed a bright red fingernail at her adoring husband. 'Did you have something to do with this, snookums?'

Jodie looked to snookums, who was sitting in a chair in the front room, mooning over his wife.

'Well, you were moping so much on the cruise at the thought that she might not be home in time for your birthday.'

Jodie felt a cold chill come over her as the pieces fell into place. 'Have you been taking your meds, Mum? Have you been resting? If you've been overdoing it on all these trips you know how stressed you can become.'

'Stressed!' Patricia pooh-poohed, turning away and heading for the comfort of the sitting room. 'These trips have been like an elixir to this old girl. Which is why Derek has bought me, wait for it…a trip to Paris for my birthday! We leave the day before Christmas Eve.' Patricia spun around with her arms outstretched like a Broadway star awaiting her applause.

Jodie looked from Derek to Patricia, dumb-struck. 'You mean that you brought me all the way here, so that we could have an early birthday celebration before you go jet-setting off to Paris?'

Derek's smile slipped away and Patricia's arms lowered, slowly and dramatically.

'I thought you might be devastated to miss seeing me before Christmas, darling. I know how much you always loved our Christmases together. We thought this would be a nice surprise.'

'Oh, rubbish!' Jodie slumped against the gaudy antique hallstand so as to keep herself upright. 'I can't believe I fell for it. I can't believe I didn't see this coming from a mile away, and, Derek, I can't believe you stooped to her level! By my coming here I may very well have lost the most important thing that has ever happened to me.'

'Your marriage visa?' Patricia spat, throwing the words at her as if she were talking about a particularly awful brand of pond scum.

'You knew about that?'

Louise. She must have heard it from Louise. Sweet Lou who, despite the little hints Jodie had given her about her childhood, would never have thought that Jodie hadn't even told her mother the good news before telling anyone else.

'You knew about that and you didn't even call me? Write to me? Ask me?' *And you wonder why I needed to go to such an extent to get away from you!*

But none of that mattered. Not now. Now what mattered was her life from this moment on. What mattered was that Jodie was no longer the mouse to be played with by the lioness.

'No, Mum,' she said, staring Patricia down, 'by coming here, I may very well have put indelible strain on my *marriage*. I left my husband behind, having to leave him a note telling him where I was as he was out of contact, all so that I could come here, to make sure you—'

She jabbed a finger towards her shocked

mother. 'To make sure you weren't about to have a nervous breakdown because you—'

She spun about and stared down the barrel of her pointed finger at Derek, who was blinking furiously. 'You intimated you were in a mad-flap panic about her health.'

'Don't blame Derek, darling. I wanted you here,' Patricia said, doing her best to pout adorably, which on a fifty-three-year-old woman with a home perm came across as ridiculous. 'And he wanted me happy. What's so bad about that?'

'What's so bad? The fact that I was not put on this earth to merely take care of your every whim. Whereas Derek made the choice to do so, and for that I will for ever be grateful.' She turned back to Derek with a shaky smile, lowering her voice and doing her best to show him she was not about to knock off his head.

'But my choice is to stay in Australia with my husband, whom I love so very much it hurts me to be away from him. And now I have gone and stuffed everything up so very badly. Even if he does understand why I left so quickly, it is likely I will not be allowed back into Australia to be with him, since my visa is about to run out and as yet I have not been issued a new one.'

Jodie moved to the front door and struggled to

load herself up with her quickly packed together bags. 'Is there something so bad about that?'

'Nothing, darling,' Patricia said, all pouting behind her. 'Nothing at all. You're right. We were wrong. We have been terribly wicked. Let me know who to call and I will do all in my power to make them let you back in the country.'

Jodie slumped beneath the weight of her mental exhaustion. 'There's no one to call, Mum. I broke the rules, and I will pay the consequences. Though I would love to blame you for evermore for it, I know that it was as much my fault for flying here at the first sign of trouble when I should have stuck to my guns and forced you guys to take care of yourselves.'

She hitched her bags higher on her shoulder and headed for the door. 'I'm leaving.'

'Where are you going?' Patricia asked. 'It's pouring out.'

'I don't know. Louise's?'

Patricia glanced away.

'The half-sister I never knew anything about? All those years when you told me that I had no one in the world but you. I would put money on the fact that you knew exactly where she was all this time. Those Christmas bonuses you received from jobs I knew you had been fired from months before. That was from the Valentines, wasn't it?'

Patricia's eyes narrowed, and her shoulders squared, and Jodie felt her pulse quicken in response. What the heck was she doing, purposely rousing the beast?

'No, sweetie, it wasn't,' Patricia said, her face turning pink. 'I was eighteen when I gave her up and I never knew what happened to her until I came home to find her letter. The *money* was from *your* father. Why do you think I spent it on trips to Chelsea and those ridiculous gardens? Because of your silly football club and your silly daffodils.'

Jodie was speechless. There was just too much new information there for her to soak it all in— the quaver in her mother's voice when talking of Louise, and the money that was from *her* father... She didn't even have the heart to chastise her mum for calling her beloved football team silly.

But then Derek held out a hand and touched Patricia gently on the back. 'Pet, come now. Let's all be friends. Now little Jodie's here let's do as we planned and have a little tipple and cheese and crackers for supper. Don't go, love,' Derek said to Jodie. 'Stay. At least tonight. And if we can get you on a plane tomorrow and back to your man, we will. I'll even pay your way.'

'Derek,' Patricia warned, and Jodie bit her lip to stop herself. Patricia couldn't help it. Her selfishness had been stoked for far too long to expect her to change now.

'Patty, shush. Jodie is all grown up and married now, and it is obvious to us all that she misses her man something terrible. And since all we want is for her to be happy, we will do all we can to make it so.'

'Sure. Of course, darling. That's all we want.'

Jodie gave Derek a grateful smile, which she managed to slide by Patricia. 'Okay, thanks, Derek. I could do with a lie-down.'

'And a cup of tea?'

'Sure. That would be nice.'

'And a piece of cake? It's sugar-free.'

She readied herself to say no as she had for so very many years. But at that moment, with all the sugar from her binge having been expelled from her system through nervous energy, a piece of cake sounded really nice. Even sugar-free cake.

'Sure, Derek. A piece of cake would go down well.'

Jodie shuffled her bags higher onto her shoulder and trudged down the hall to the spare room with its small, lumpy single bed. Derek had money for trips, but somehow this spare bed had never been upgraded. Priorities. His priorities were about making Patricia happy.

Being here, in London, Jodie finally knew what her priorities were. Tomorrow she would ring the embassy, she would book herself a flight, and if she had to grapple with the flight attendant to get herself on that plane, she would.

Appearances be damned, because she was a girl no longer displaced. She was a girl who wanted nothing more than to go home.

Jodie was roused from her open-eyed rest on the lumpiest bed in the world when a knock came at the front door. Derek was taking a nap and Patricia was…well, Patricia, so Jodie dragged her weary bones from her bed and shuffled down the hall to answer it.

Jodie opened the door to her mother's humble flat to find… 'Heath!'

Her heart rocketed thunderously in her chest. Of all the people she would have expected to be face to face with in that moment, Heath would have ranked a few places below both Santa and Elvis.

But there he was, decked out in jeans and a deep red jumper and an old brown leather jacket and a really old scarf that looked as though it had been in storage for a number of years. To cap off the bizarre picture of him wearing all his clothes at once, the rain pelted down in a sheet of molten silver at his back. Against such a perfectly English backdrop he looked even more tanned, even more gorgeous, and even more…

'Heath,' she repeated as she stepped out onto the balcony and half closed the door behind her. 'What are you doing here?'

A wry grin creased his beautiful face. 'Well, that's not exactly the welcome I was hoping for. True, it's the one I was expecting, but not the one I was hoping for.'

Jodie just stared at him, still trying to reconcile the fact that he was there, in London, at her mother's home, just a few hours after she herself had arrived.

'Can I come in?' Heath asked, and only then did Jodie notice he was shivering.

'Of course,' she said, reaching out and taking him by one wet arm and pulling him inside. She ran her hand up his arm and hooked her hand under the strap of his bag and slid it to a patch of floor against the wall.

Heath shook his head, a spray of raindrops flickering the walls leaving his sun-streaked hair standing up in boyish spikes. He looked down at her then, and she noticed the dark smudges beneath his eyes. She would have put money on the fact that he'd had as little sleep since they'd parted as she had.

'You have no idea how petrified I was to come home and find you not there, Jodie,' he said at long last, his deep voice rumbling in the small musty hallway.

'I left you a note,' she said, but she knew that wouldn't have been nearly enough. If she had been in his position, if she had come home to find him gone, she would have felt torn apart. And the fact that he was there, covered in raindrops, *must* mean that he had felt the very same way.

'Mum needed me,' she explained again, redoubling the information she had put in her letter. 'I had to come.'

He reached out and ran a hand over her waves. 'I know you did, sweetheart. I know how important your family is to you. I feel the same way about mine.'

His hand moved down to cup her cheek, his skin feeling cool against her hot cheek. It was all she could do not to lean into him and purr.

'But I hope you understand that I had to come too,' he said. And then he took a firm hold on her chin and bent down and laid a soft, warm kiss upon her lips, so that she could be in no doubt of his meaning. She leant into his kiss like a leaf turning to find the sun, and her eyes clenched shut tight as she gave in to the impossible sensation of having the man of her dreams back at her side.

He pulled away first, just far enough so he could look into her eyes, and to make sure she was looking at him too.

'After spending one night away, the boys on the Run couldn't stand the sight of me moping. They insisted I go back home. When I got there, you were already gone. And there was your note, on the hall table where we had always left notes as kids.'

'I rang Elena, desperate for a way to track you down. She suggested it.'

'Really?' he asked, and Jodie heard the surprise in his voice.

'I knew it,' she said, poking him in the chest. 'You said she was happy about us, but you know she doesn't like me.'

'It's not that she doesn't like you, sweetheart. She was just afraid that in marrying you I would only end up hurt in the end. But if she told you about leaving a note on the table, I would suggest that maybe now she has come around to my way of thinking after all.'

'You must have come awfully fast after getting the note,' she said, not quite sure how to ask the other question: *Why* did you come so quickly?

'My brother Caleb works part-time on the phones for Qantas, so I rang him and insisted he get me on the next plane to London. He did, on the provision he could come with me. I left him at a hotel across the street from mine in…'

Heath pulled out a receipt for a room at a sophisticated hotel in Kensington. Jodie knew it, had walked past once or twice but had never been inside. Not even to use the bathrooms, which she had heard were opulent enough themselves.

'Who is it?' Patricia called out suddenly from the kitchenette.

Jodie took Heath by the hand, needing his warm strength to get her through what could very well be a traumatic occurrence. He pulled back, spinning her until she faced him.

'I'm really glad to see you, Jodie,' he said.

'I'm glad to see you too,' she admitted.

'Are you?'

She swallowed down her fear of rejection, of not being good enough. He had taken a leap coming here, and now it was her turn to show him how much that meant to her.

'The thought of not seeing you again, for a day, a week, for ever… That's the one thing that almost stopped me from coming.'

His beautiful blue eyes had grown dark and unfathomable, and she hoped she hadn't scared him back to the other side of the world with the depth of her need for him. But he only squeezed her hand tighter still.

'That was worth a twenty-hour flight in a seat that could barely fit a five-foot kid, much less six feet two inches of not terribly flexible grown man,' he said, his heartbreaking eyes lighting from within.

Boy, did Jodie want to kiss him right then. Really kiss him. Throw herself into his arms and kiss him until she passed out.

'Jodie!' Patricia called out. 'Was anybody there?' Patricia, the one person in the world who would put a stop to her fun. Well, not this time.

'Mum, I'm going out. I'll be back later.' She grabbed Heath's bag and dragged him out into the cold wet night.

'Where are we going?' Heath asked, but he didn't really much care. He was so happy to be with her again, she could take him wherever she pleased.

'To your hotel,' she said, pulling at his arm until he thought it might yank all the way off.

When they reached the end of the balcony, and had hit the stairs running, Heath pulled her to a stop, spinning her until her back rested against the old red brick of the stairwell to find she was shivering from top to toe.

Her jeans and fitted pink tracksuit top were perfect for inside a heated flat, but out in the wet December air she must have been freezing. Her nose was already pink, and her eyes bright with moisture from the cold.

'What about your mum?' he asked, moving in just a little closer. He ached to wrap her up so tight she couldn't feel any sensation of cold or wet. 'Is she okay?'

Her intense eyes dulled ever so slightly as she gave a small shrug. 'She's mad as a snake. And unfixable. She will continue to be that way with me there or without me there, so I have decided that I would rather be *not* there. I would rather be with you.'

She lowered her fine chin, looking up at him from beneath auburn eyelashes, just in case he didn't catch her drift. He caught it just fine. In fact certain parts of his anatomy were in absolute accord and willed him to just shut up and do as she said.

But there were things that had to be sorted out first. Falling into bed, no matter how very satisfying that would be, wouldn't solve things, wouldn't straighten out the continual emotional messes the two of them kept landing in. Their one divine night together had only proved that.

'Jodie, sweetheart. Stop. Just for a moment. We have plenty of time. A week at least. That's how far ahead I am paid up at the hotel, but if you think you would prefer to spend more time there, with me, and the king-sized bed, and the Jacuzzi and room service, that would be fine by me too.'

All signs of flirtation disappeared in a blink of her fine green eyes. 'A week? At *that* hotel?'

He nodded, taking her hands and drawing her a little closer again so he could rub some warmth into her now-shaking arms.

'But Christmas is only a couple of days away.'

'Tell me about it. I thought inner-city Melbourne hotel prices could be steep, but you try finding a decent hotel, with a honeymoon suite, in London, this close to the silly season.'

Her wide eyes flickered back and forth between his as the words 'honeymoon suite' sank in. And he couldn't help but smile when he saw her tuck those words away to focus on other, less-confronting issues.

'But what about your family?' she asked. 'Elena told me that everyone is coming to the Run for Christmas.'

He shrugged. 'They always do. And no doubt they still will. But I won't be there.'

'But…what…how…why?'

Unable to stop himself any longer, he pulled her hips away from the wall so he could fully wrap his arms around her small waist until he felt as if he were hugging himself. 'Jodie, I *plan* on being with the most important member of my family for Christmas. You, my sweet, stubborn bride, are it.'

'I am?'

'Yes, wife, you are.'

Heath lifted her left hand and kissed her knuckle just below her wedding ring. The ring with the intertwined flowers indicative of their very different beginnings. The ring that symbolised the union of their two very different sensibilities, personalities, and souls. The ring that he hoped so very much would remain on that pale, tapered finger until the end of time.

'They'll all hate me for taking you away from them,' she said, obviously still not quite believing what she was hearing. Well, he would just have to tell her again and again and again until he cracked through that time-hardened shell of self-doubt.

'Sweetheart, they'll *love* you for taking me away. For too many years I have been the cantankerous big brother working too hard, living out his life at the old family farm while they got on with making their own families.'

'They'll love me?' she said.

'And they're not the only ones.'

'They're not?'

'Mmm. Mandy and Lisa are missing you like crazy. When I rang them to find your mum's address and to tell them I was coming here to get you, they made sure I brought a tub of Vegemite for you.'

'Vegemite? I hate Vegemite.'

'Really? Okay, so maybe Mandy and Lisa don't love you as much as they enjoy torturing you.'

'Right.' She bit at her inner lip for a few seconds before bucking up and asking the one question Heath had been waiting for, counting on, needing, to push him over the edge once and for all. 'Anyone else?'

'Well, even your crazy mother loves you enough to want you home to celebrate her birthday. And Derek loved you enough to set you free in the first place.'

'Mmm, I guess. Though I'm not sure I am ready to give them the benefit of the doubt as yet.'

As they stared into one another's eyes she began to shiver in earnest, her slight body trembling in his arms. He ran his hands up and down her back, and she let him do so without protest and he wondered whether she was really as cold as she was making out.

'And there's someone else,' he said, realising he didn't care about her motives for snuggling up to him as he was enjoying the fact of it so very much. 'I'm sure of it; I just can't think who...'

Unable to stand the waiting any longer, Jodie finally gave into her impatience and slapped him on the chest. 'Spit it out, Heath, or I might divorce you and stay here after all.'

'Oh, that's right, it's me. I love you.'

And no matter how flippant the delivery of the words, the sparkling eyes and grin that accompanied them, Jodie was completely floored. Her hand went lax against his chest before curling tightly into a hunk of red wool.

Heath loved her.

No matter how hard her belted self-esteem and her niggling subconscious tried to find a way to twist his words, they could not.

Heath loved her!

And she loved him. So much her heart felt as if it were about to burst. Especially because she knew that her love for him didn't take away any of the regard she had for herself—it was good for her, nurtured her, and made her a better person.

'There's more I need to say.'

More than the fact that he loved her? Jodie wasn't sure she could handle more.

'A few weeks ago,' he began, 'I had a scare when a close friend of mine passed away. I realised in that moment that my life was passing me by with no one to witness it. I had no particular someone to miss me when I'm gone. But since being with you, I have come to realise that it's about having someone to *share* your life. I want you, Jodie, to share my life for evermore as I want to share yours. And I was kind of hoping you might feel the same way.'

And she realised that, though the words had been living inside her, filling her, warming her for days, weeks even, she had never once said them out loud. And rather than the thought incapacitating her, the words leapt to the tip of her tongue and onwards.

'Heath, I love you so much it hurts. I love you so much I think of little else when you're not with me. I love you so much that somehow in the back of my mind I believed that even by coming here and breaking the terms of my visa my love would be strong enough to keep us together.'

'Yours and mine,' he said, sneaking in close enough to kiss her on the tip of her nose.

'But what if I can't go home?' she asked. Home. Jamesons Run—the place in the world where she felt more like herself than any other.

Heath moved away, too far for her comfort, but only far enough to reach inside his jacket pocket. He pulled out a crumpled letter, which had been opened and returned to its envelope. She knew, without even looking at the return address, what it was.

'My Temporary Spouse Visa,' she whispered.

'Your Temporary Spouse Visa,' he said.

'I got it?'

'You got it.'

'Oh. Oh, my. Oh, how wonderful. Oh, no! Didn't Mr Cage say that I had to be in Australia when I received it? Don't tell me how badly I have ruined everything!'

'Well, if you shut up and let me get a word in for once I can tell you how badly you've ruined everything.'

Jodie bit her lip and looked up into Heath's beautiful blue eyes and wished with all her might that it weren't irrevocably badly.

'Since so many people back home love you so very much,' Heath said, 'and even though you did your best to wreck your big chance, you haven't even managed to ruin a thing. When I called Mandy, and explained what you had gone and done, she called Scott. And Scott called his pal Malcolm Cage. Any time you wish to come back into the country after our honeymoon is fine with the Australian Department of Immigration.'

'Scott? Scott did this for us?'

'That he did. For a funny little bloke, he sure came through for you in the end. He loves you in his own way too.'

'Ha! Mandy can barely look him in the eye, but I always knew there was more to him than a fondness for mesh and leather,' she said, all but under her breath. And she knew she couldn't wait to get back home to give the little guy a great big hug. But first she had another guy whom she wanted to hug and kiss a whole lot more.

'Did you really say honeymoon suite?' she asked, tucking the letter back into Heath's jacket.

'With a Jacuzzi built for two.'

'But didn't you say Caleb is here too?'

'Yep. In his own room, at a budget hotel across

the street, which he is paying for out of his own pocket. I've decided that now I am a married man with marriage-type concerns of my own, my extended family might have to start looking out for themselves a little bit more.'

'I like the sound of that very much,' she said, snuggling closer and closer, wrapping herself in his scent and the feel of his warm body so very close to hers.

'Jodie?'

Jodie fair leapt out of her skin when she saw her mother's head poke around the corner of the staircase. 'Mum! What are you doing here?'

'I wondered where you had gone.'

Jodie pulled herself around Heath to stand in between him and her mother, who had thrown of all things a matted old fur coat over her clothes before heading out.

'Um, Mum. This is Heath Jameson. My husband.'

'Oh,' Patricia said, her eyes opening wide.

Heath leaned around Jodie and held out a wide tanned hand. As Patricia always did around a handsome man, she all but curtsied as she gave him a limp ladylike handshake.

'Pleased to meet you, Patricia.'

'Likewise, I'm sure.' Patricia managed to drag her eyes from Heath's handsome face long enough to remember Jodie was even there. Jodie braced herself for some sort of passive-aggressive comment.

'Won't you both come inside?' Patricia said. 'Stay for a drink. Derek and I would really like it if you would.'

Jodie froze. That was it? Heath gave her waist a little squeeze, and she knew he would follow her lead whatever she decided to do.

The temptation of the hotel, the king-sized bed and the Jacuzzi was strong. But a civilized drink with Derek, Patricia, and her new husband? Somehow she thought this would be a night that might never in her life be repeated.

'Okay, Mum. We'll stay.'

That night, they had a party enlivened by cheap champagne—Jodie did her best not to monitor how much her mum drank—and canapés with some sort of smear on top that tasted vaguely fishy. They all wore paper party hats, and feather boas, with Patricia's being the most vibrant red.

Patricia was an utterly eccentric hostess. Derek mooned over her every move. And Heath and Jodie sat back and watched the whole thing as if it were some sort of anthropological experiment.

'They are madly in love, aren't they?' Heath

whispered into Jodie's ear as Patricia fed Derek from a bunch of grapes.

'Yeah,' Jodie agreed. 'Even a year down the track they look like honeymooners.'

'Do you think we'll be like them when we get old and grey?'

'Don't count on it, buddy!' she said, laughing. 'But then again, the day Patricia lets herself turn grey I'll feed you anything you like.'

Christmas Day dawned rainy and grey.

Jodie peeked out of the curtains to the London street five floors below, and took in what was maybe her last British Christmas for a good long while. But that didn't really matter. So long as she and her husband were together, the Christmases could be white, golden, or hot pink with green spots as far as she was concerned.

Jodie took a big long sip of lukewarm black tea, deciding that, though it was hardly exotic, this was in fact her favourite drink. Especially since her husband had made it for her.

The bed rocked and Jodie smiled as she felt Heath slide back under the sheets after ordering room service.

'Good morning, wife,' he whispered before nibbling on her ear.

She let the curtain fall back into place, then

rolled until she lay beneath him, and sighed as he settled into a more comfortable position with his legs curled along hers.

'Good morning, husband,' she said, tracing a finger along his clean-cut jaw.

'Plans for today?'

'Um, I was thinking of lying in for a bit. Eating something rich, sweet, and decadent. A dip in the tub followed by lunch. Then maybe some more time lying in.'

'And as for the rest of the day?'

'Your choice.'

'Hmm,' he hummed into her neck. 'I'm sure I can come up with something to keep us occupied.'

Jodie gave into the heady sensation for a few moments longer before the buzzing in her head grew too loud. Though it pained her to do so, she pushed Heath away. 'But first I have to make a phone call.'

Heath's eyebrows raised in surprise. 'To whom?'

'Lou. I'll be quick, I promise. I've had an idea in my head the last couple of days and I won't rest until I follow it through.'

'You won't rest?' Heath asked. 'You've talked to her on the phone every day since you've been here. Please don't tell your new husband that your lack of rest has more to do with this idea in your head than to do with his energetic and improvisational lovemaking?'

She kissed him quickly on the mouth. 'I would never tell you that.'

'Why, you little—'

But Jodie had already reached out for the phone and begun to dial. She held a finger to her lips, demanding he be quiet.

He grinned down at her, his heavenly blue eyes brimming with devilment, and she had the distinct feeling that the second she was off the phone she would have to pay for her dissidence. The very thought had her wanting to get off the phone as soon as humanly possible.

'Louise Valentine speaking.'

'Merry Christmas!'

'Merry Christmas, Jodie. And thanks so much for the present.'

'Promise me you'll wear it today.'

'Oh, I have every intention of doing so. I am meeting the Valentines for our regular Christmas do later today, which ought to be a stilted and uncomfortable family affair as per usual, and this will set off my outfit perfectly.'

'That's my girl.' Jodie grinned, though she thought it more likely the flashing mistletoe belly ring would end up hidden beneath some elegant ensemble in the end. 'Now, before you make another excuse as to why we haven't caught up, don't panic. I have a way you can make it up to me.'

Heath suddenly disappeared beneath the sheets at the end of the bed.

'Oh,' Louise said. 'And what would that be, now?'

'You need a date for this big Valentine Christmas party, right? Well, I think I have just the guy in mind. Heath's brother Caleb. He's blond. He's a surfer. He's gorgeous. He's twenty-seven and he's looking for someone to show him around. And he is just the sort to drive your dread cousin Max mad, which would surely make the party that much more fun for you. I am giving him your number.'

Caleb had begged them to take him out to dinner every night since they'd been there. And though the spate of fabulous restaurants they had frequented, including the magnificent Bella Lucia flagship restaurant in Jodie's beloved Chelsea, were really very nice, she would prefer scrambled eggs with Heath in her hotel room any night.

Louise's pause spoke volumes. 'Me? My number?'

'Yes, you. Single, workaholic, has had no dates since I have known you. Take him to the party. Introduce him to Cosmopolitans. Show him the London Eye. Okay?'

'Well, I guess… Okay.'

Jodie pulled her foot away as Heath began to tickle it in earnest. 'I have to go, Lou. Talk to you later,' she said, before hanging up and throwing the phone onto the carpet.

She pulled her feet up to her chest and tried her best to roll away, but Heath grabbed her around the waist and pulled her deeper under the covers with him. She came face to face with him, the glow of the morning sun shining through the white cotton sheet.

'No more phone calls,' Heath said, his voice deep and suggestive and sending tingles all the way to Jodie's toes that felt way better than tickling ever could.

'No more phone calls,' she promised before giving in and kissing her husband.

But come on, she was in love, and she only wished the whole world were as happy. Was that such a bad thing?

* * * * *

Next month The Brides of Bella Lucia *saga
continues in*
Married Under the Mistletoe
by
Linda Goodnight

*Daniel has just arrived in London, having
discovered that his long-lost father is John
Valentine. Now, at the exclusive Knightsbridge
Bella Lucia restaurant, Daniel may have finally met his match in beautiful manager
Stephanie Ellison—but does he have the
power to break down Stephanie's barriers?*

STEPHANIE SQUEEZED out yet another mop full of water and watched in dismay as more seeped from beneath the industrial-sized dishwasher. She'd called the plumber again about this a week ago and still he had yet to show up. Ordinarily, she'd have followed up and called someone else, but she'd had too many other problems on her mind. One, the money missing from the Bella Lucia accounts—something that, as restaurant manager, she would have to sort out soon.

Two, Daniel Stephens. Since the moment he'd arrived, the man had occupied her thoughts in the most uncomfortable way. Then he'd taken her on that picnic and she'd realized why. She liked him. His passion for Africa stirred her. His relentless pursuit of an incredibly lofty goal stirred her. Looking at him stirred her.

A voice that also stirred her broke through the sound of sloshing water. "Ahoy, mate. Permission to come aboard."

Stephanie looked up. All she could think was, *Ohmygosh. Ohmygosh.*

She'd known he was coming. She'd been expecting him. But she hadn't been expecting this.

Barefoot and shirtless, Daniel waded toward her in a pair of low slung jeans, a tool belt slung even lower on his trim hips.

Close your mouth, Stephanie. Mop, don't stare.

But she stared anyway.

Daniel Stephens, dark as sin, chest and shoulder muscles rippling, black hair still wet and carelessly slicked back from a pirate's forehead was almost enough to make her forget the reasons why she could not be interested in him. Almost.

Slim hips rolling, he sloshed through the quarter inch of water to the dishwasher. Dark hairs sprinkled his bare toes.

The sight made her shiver. When had she ever paid any attention to a man's toes?

"You forgot your shirt," she blurted, repeating the slogan seen everywhere in American restaurants. "No shirt, no shoes, no service."

He grinned at her, unrepentant. "You said you needed me. *Badly.* How could I not respond immediately to that kind of plea from a beautiful woman?"

He thought she was beautiful? The idea stunned

her. Beautiful? Something inside her shriveled. How little he knew about the real her.

He, on the other hand, was hot. And he knew it.

"Are you going to fix that thing or annoy me?"

One corner of his mouth twitched. "Both, I imagine."

He hunkered down in front of the washer, tool belt dragging the waist of his jeans lower. Stephanie tried not to look.

"Do you think it's bad?"

"Probably have to shut down the restaurant for a week."

Stephanie dropped the mop. It clattered to the floor. "You've got to be kidding!"

He twisted around on those sexy bare toes and said, "I am. It's probably a leaky hose."

"Can you fix it?"

He smirked. "Of course."

"Then I really am going to fire that plumber."

"Go ahead and sack the useless lout. Tell him you have an engineer around to do your midnight bidding."

Now, *that* was an intriguing thought.

She retrieved the mop. "Which is more expensive? A plumber or an engineer?"

White teeth flashed. "Depends on what you use for payment."

Time to shut up, Stephanie, before you get in too deep. Do not respond to that tempting innuendo.

Metal scraped against tile as he easily manhandled the large machine, walking it away from the cabinet to look inside and behind. Stephanie went back to swabbing the decks. Watching Daniel, all muscled and half naked, was too dangerous. Thinking about that cryptic payment remark was even more so.

"Could you lend a hand over here?" he asked.

Oh dear.

The floor, dangerously slick but no longer at flood stage, proved to be an adventure. But she slip-slid her way across to where Daniel bent over, peering into the back of the machine.

"What can I do?"

"See this space?"

Seeing required Stephanie to move so close to Daniel that his warm, soap-scented and very nude skin brushed against her. Thankful for long sleeves, she swallowed hard and tried to focus on the space in question.

"Down there where that black thing is?" she asked.

"Your hands are small enough, I think, to loosen that screw. Do you see it?"

"I think so." She leaned farther into the

machine, almost lying across the top. Daniel's warm purr directed her, too close to her ear, but necessary to get the job done.

"That's it. Good girl."

His praise pleased her, silly as that seemed.

He pressed in closer, trying to reach the now unfastened hose. His breath puffed deliciously against the side of her neck. Stephanie shivered and gave up trying to ignore the sensation.

Their fingers touched, deep inside the machine. Both of them stilled.

Her pulse escalating to staccato, Stephanie's blood hummed. As if someone else controlled her actions, she turned her head and came face to face with searing blue eyes that surely saw to her deepest secrets.

She needed to move, to get out of this situation and put space between them. But she was trapped between the machine, the hose, and Daniel's inviting, compelling body.

"I think I have it," she said, uselessly. Foolishly.

Daniel's nostrils flared. "Yes. You certainly do."

His lips spoke so close to hers that she almost felt kissed.

Daniel held her gaze for another long, pulsing moment in which Stephanie began to yearn for the touch of his lips against hers. How would they feel?

All right, she told herself. That's enough. Stop right now before you venture too close to the fire and get burned.

With the inner strength that had kept her going when life had been unspeakable, she withdrew her hand and stepped away.

As though the air between them hadn't throbbed like jungle drums, Daniel didn't bother to look up. He finished repairing the hose while Stephanie completed the mopping up and tried to analyze the situation. Daniel was interested in her. Big deal. In her business, she got hit on all the time.

But it wasn't Daniel's interest that bothered her so much. It was her own. Something in Daniel drew her, called to her like a Siren's song. One moment he was cynical and tough. The next he was giving and gentle. There was a strength in him, too, that said he could and would move a mountain if one was in his way. He was different from anyone she'd ever met.

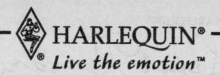

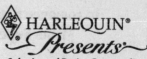

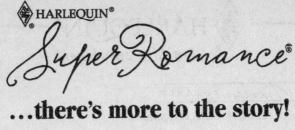
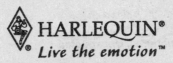

Harlequin® Historical
Historical Romantic Adventure!

Imagine a time of chivalrous knights and unconventional ladies, roguish rakes and impetuous heiresses, rugged cowboys and spirited frontierswomen— these rich and vivid tales will capture your imagination!

Harlequin Historical... they're too good to miss!

HARLEQUIN®
Presents

The world's bestselling romance series...
The series that brings you your favorite authors,
month after month:

Helen Bianchin...Emma Darcy
Lynne Graham...Penny Jordan
Miranda Lee...Sandra Marton
Anne Mather...Carole Mortimer
Susan Napier...Michelle Reid

and many more uniquely talented authors!

Wealthy, powerful, gorgeous men...
Women who have feelings just like your own...
The stories you love, set in exotic, glamorous locations...

HARLEQUIN®
Presents

Seduction and Passion Guaranteed!

2 Love Inspired novels and 2 mystery gifts... Absolutely FREE!

Visit
www.LoveInspiredBooks.com
for your two FREE books, sent directly to you!

BONUS: Choose between regular print or our NEW larger print format!

There's no catch! You're under no obligation to buy anything. We charge nothing—ZERO—for your first shipment. And you don't have to make any minimum number of purchases.

You'll like the convenience of home delivery at our special discount prices, and you'll love your free subscription to Steeple Hill News, our members-only newsletter.

We hope that after receiving your free books, you'll want to remain a subscriber. But the choice is yours—to continue or cancel, anytime at all! So why not take us up on our invitation, with no risk of any kind!